Truelove Hills

PATRINA McKENNA

Copyright © 2019 Patrina McKenna

All rights reserved

This book is a work of fiction. Names, characters, places, and incidents either are products of the author's imagination or are used fictitiously. Any resemblance to actual persons, living or dead, events, or locales is entirely coincidental.

Publisher: Patrina McKenna

patrina.mckenna@outlook.com

ISBN-13: 978-0-9932624-5-6

Also by Patrina McKenna

The GIANT GEMSTONES series
Feel good fantasy for all the family!

(in reading order)

GIANT Gemstones
A Galaxy of Gemstones
The Gemstone Dynasty
Enrico's Journey
Summer Camp at Tadgers Blaney Manor

The TRUELOVE HILLS series
Romantic comedy with a twist!

(in reading order)

Truelove Hills
Truelove Hills – Mystery at Pebble Cove
Truelove Hills – The Matchmaker

DEDICATION

For my family and friends

PROLOGUE

Christmas Eve, 1999

To My Darling Daughters,

When you're old enough to read this letter, you will know that the cruel twist of fate that took me from you wasn't so bad, time is a healer, and the memories we made are forever to hold. Your strong, loving family will teach you right from wrong, let you fly as high as you desire and wipe your tears when you fall.

Hannah – You were ten when we parted and will remember me most. You look so much like your father with your black curly hair and green eyes. All the signs at school are that you will excel in whatever you choose to do. The world is at your feet, Hannah, please take it in both hands and let nothing or no-one hold you back.

Matilda – At six years old you are loving and caring and doing well with your reading. You always have your nose in a book! You're also the only one of my daughters with blue eyes; my eyes. I wish you a life full of happiness and fulfilment and that whatever path you venture down is the right one; only you will know when it's right.

Tabitha and Tallulah – Just eighteen months old, our time together was way too short. You have your grandmother to thank for your lovely red hair, and when you look into your grandfather's bright green eyes you will see the resemblance in your own; you are Makepeace girls, through and through. I am sure that Pebblestown will be a better place having you both as part of its community – double the trouble, double the fun! Your future is bright my darlings.

It's time for me to go now, you will all remain forever in my heart.

Your loving Mother xxxx

(Harriet Makepeace)

David Makepeace handed the tearstained letter to his mother, Alice, before his shaking shoulders gave way to violent, uncontrollable sobs.

'Oh, David, it's such a tragedy that's fallen upon us; Harriet was so young.' Alice embraced her only son and willed all her strength to pass through to the broken man he'd become.

Arthur wiped his eyes and vowed to be strong for the family. David and Alice would need him, although those poor girls would need him more.

Alice ushered Arthur into the hallway of the Solent Sea Guest House. 'We'll tell the girls when they wake up in the morning.'

Arthur stared at his strong, loving wife. Her beautiful red hair was now tinged with silver, she'd kept it long all her life, Arthur had refused to let her cut it. 'There'll be no retirement for us now, Alice, we have to keep the family together. David and the children need us. It'll be difficult at our age, but we'll have to bring those girls up as our own.'

'What are you waffling on about Arthur Makepeace? Our granddaughters are our own. There's no couple better equipped to raise them. We're only in our sixties; there's lots of life left in us yet.'

Arthur sighed. 'Tomorrow's Christmas Day.'

Alice lowered her eyes. 'I know. We'll get through tomorrow as best as we can and then we'll make sure that every Christmas is extra special for the girls. Christmas is such a magical time of year; we need to keep it that way.'

Arthur nodded. Alice was his rock – their lives were entwined. They were both born in Pebblestown, in the same class at school and married at nineteen. Theirs was the love of a lifetime, and between them, they'd do their best for their family.

Arthur hugged his wife. 'I love you, Alice Makepeace.'

Tears streamed down Alice's face and she wiped them with the back of her hand. 'I know you do, Arthur Makepeace. I love you too.'

1

THE EXTRAORDINARY MEETING

February, 2019

'I'd like to welcome everyone to tonight's extraordinary meeting.' The chairman coughed, and the buttons on his waistcoat severed a thread or two of the expensive black cotton keeping them in place.

'This meeting has been called in addition to our scheduled programme of parish council meetings for this year.'

The chairman cleared his throat again and reached for the water pitcher. His mug already contained a good slug of whisky. He hadn't got to where he was today without a secret or two. These meetings were always dull, and a little tipple kept him alert. Water poured into his mug and a nice gulp to ease the guilty tickle worked wonders.

'Now, as we have a new member on the committee. I suggest we all introduce ourselves. Let's start with Lady Lovett on my left.'

Lady Lovett patted her high blonde bun before standing with hands on hips. 'I am Lady Leticia Lovett, and I live in Chateau Amore de Pebblio. I have to categorically state that it will be an absolute travesty if we do not reach agreement this evening to change the name of our village.' The lady sat down and folded her arms before glaring at the elderly gentleman next to her.

'My name's Arthur Makepeace. I'm a retired stonemason. The name of this village will change over my dead body.'

Arthur turned to the young man on his left. 'My name is Theo Tressler. I'm a photographer. I moved to the village last week. I must admit I'm surprised, but delighted, to be invited to join the parish council.'

Theo smiled at the young woman next to him. 'You all know who I am, but for Theo's sake, my name's Cindy Copperfield. I own Cindy's Bakery.'

The Chairman nudged the man to his right. 'My name is David Makepeace. I'm proprietor of the Solent Sea fully-licensed Guest House.'

The Chairman rose to his feet. 'I'm Edgar Trueman, international businessman and Chair of the parish council. There's one item on the agenda tonight, and that's the re-naming of our village from Pebblestown to Truelove Hills. All those in favour say "aye".'

Theo Tressler waved his hand in the air. 'Excuse me. Could you please outline the reason for the name change?'

Lady Lovett leant forward. 'Isn't it obvious? Who wants to come to a place called Pebblestown?'

Cindy backed the Lady up. 'Truelove Hills sounds much more romantic than Pebblestown. Just imagine all the couples wanting to stay at the Solent Sea Guest House. We definitely need to bring tourists to the area. We live in such a pretty part of England, yet no-one ever visits. We're off the beaten track. By changing the name, it could be a romantic hideaway for couples in love.'

Theo made notes. He had another question: 'Why Truelove Hills, why not just Truelove?'

Edgar wasn't in the mood for a debate. He'd invited the photographer thinking he'd be a pushover like Cindy. He downed the contents of his mug before smiling through gritted teeth. 'As a seasoned traveller, I have identified the potential this village has to offer. We have hills, lots of them. People go to places with hills. Just think about Beverley Hills and Hollywood

Hills. We can't miss an opportunity by leaving the Hills part off.'

Lady Lovett was becoming agitated. How could this young whippersnapper question the ideas of the staunch members of the parish? 'Edgar and Miss Copperfield both have relevant points. For my part, I am keen to add a continental slant to our future marketing campaigns. We should promote our village as the English version of Provence or Tuscany; a picturesque hideaway in the south of England. I have named my mansion accordingly. I will be taking guests and hosting functions at Chateau Amore de Pebblio.' David Makepeace shifted in his chair.

Theo sent Lady Lovett a flash of shiny white teeth. A dimple adorned his right cheek, and his dark brown eyes twinkled as he ran his hands through his tousled brown hair. He leant back in his chair. 'I like your style, Lady Lovett. There's no doubt the continental slant would bring visitors to the area. I'm not sure about the proposed name change though. One cannot deny the fact that the village's charm comes from the pebble buildings, lanes and rockery formations amongst the hills.'

The Lady blushed. Theo connected with her on a very deep level. Arthur Makepeace clapped his hands three times. 'About time! You've hit the nail on the head young man. It's all about the pebbles.'

The Chairman banged his fist on the table. 'I will ask again. All those in favour of changing our village name from Pebblestown to Truelove Hills say "aye".'

There were three affirmations . . . and a delayed fourth. David Makepeace dropped his head as his father's eyes pierced through him.

Edgar Trueman rubbed his hands together. 'Decision made. I will agree an action plan with Lady Lovett and copy you all in. There will need to be a naming ceremony and then we can advertise everything there is to offer in Truelove Hills. Tourists will be flocking here by the summer. There's no time to waste. Meeting closed.'

Arthur rose from his chair and shuffled to the door. He may as well be dead. He would never speak to his only son again. In fact, he would never speak to anyone else ever again in a million years; he'd just go home to rot.

Edgar shook hands with David Makepeace. 'That was a close call. I got that outsider to join the committee to sway the vote. Didn't think he'd fold like that. Shame you had to go against your old man.'

David Makepeace sighed. A change of name and the promotion to go with it would do wonders for his business. His father was sulking now, but he'd get over it.

Arthur pushed open the door to his cottage. He didn't bother locking it. He never had. He touched the pebble walls to steady himself as he made his way to his seat by the window. He could see the world from that seat. His world – the only world he ever needed. He knew everything that went on in Pebblestown. How could his son be so ignorant? They were planning a takeover bid that Edgar Trueman and Lady Lovett. It was all about the pebbles. Always had been; always would be.

2

THE NEW RESIDENT

Theo Tressler didn't have a studio. He had a website, a camera and a small rented apartment above the Post Office & General Store. He was surprised that no-one had queried his meagre existence. He was even more taken aback when Mrs Carruthers had advised him that Edgar Trueman suggested he join the parish council. She'd said, 'Businessmen are in short supply around these parts.'

Theo wondered why Mrs Carruthers wasn't on the council herself. She managed the Post Office & General Store. Still, it wasn't for him to query these things. He was delighted to have been embraced by the community almost as soon as his black patent leather shoes skidded on the pebble-studded doorstep of Mrs Carruthers' shop. Another job to do; packing more sensible shoes hadn't been a priority before leaving London. London . . . that seemed a lifetime ago, yet it had been less than a month since he'd made the snap decision to move to Pebblestown.

Reaching into his briefcase, Theo removed a photocopy of a newspaper article. It was dated eighty years ago, and next to a photograph of a young boy the words read:

> *Schoolboy, Arthur Makepeace, aged seven, has won a competition to re-name a village. He said, 'I want my village to be called Pebblestown. It's all about the pebbles.' The judging panel agreed wholeheartedly with Arthur. The naming ceremony will take place on the 1st of March in the village square.*

Theo sat down at his desk. His apartment overlooked the High Street and was directly opposite Arthur's small cottage. The old man could be seen sitting watching the world go by from his living room window. He'd been there every day since the Extraordinary Meeting. Theo had heard from Mrs Carruthers that Arthur was refusing to communicate with the outside world. His son, David, had placed an order at the General Store for the home delivery of groceries and came in daily to pay the bill.

When Theo popped into the bakery for croissants the next morning Cindy suggested he stayed for a pot of tea and a chat. It was cosy inside the bakery; there were just three small tables covered with red and white gingham cloths. Cindy said she had some wrought iron tables and chairs to put outside in the better weather. It was February now though, and she was keen to keep the door to her business shut. Theo knew the conversation was going to turn serious when she turned the 'OPEN' sign to 'CLOSED' and locked the door.

Tears clouded Cindy's eyes. 'I'm very upset about Arthur. My heart goes out to him. He's not left his cottage for days. It was terrible having to vote against him at the meeting, but this village needs bringing back to life. I was born here, and it used to have a tremendous community spirit. Unfortunately, there's no work for people around here. All my friends have moved elsewhere, even my parents have retired to Spain. David Makepeace has been very supportive of me. He always pops in for rolls and croissants for his guest house. I think it's because his daughter Matilda has asked him to. We were best friends at school. I miss her so much. When her grandmother died, she went away to university. She was very close to her grandparents after losing her mother when she was six.'

Theo offered Cindy more tea from the pot.

Cindy sighed and grabbed the young man's hand. 'It's so sad when people can't move with the times. Just look around. How many people are there in this shop?'

Theo retrieved his hand back. 'Well, it does say "CLOSED".'

Cindy shook her head. 'That makes no difference. I'll see a handful of people today. I can't keep my business afloat. I only started it up last summer. People used to get their bread and cakes from the General Store before. I spend most afternoons throwing crumbs to the birds or going up to Pebble Peak to feed the ducks on the lake. You could always come to Pebble Peak with me if you like. What about this afternoon?'

Theo sighed, why were girls always so keen to spend time with him? He needed to keep Cindy at bay. 'I'll be working this afternoon. I work every afternoon, and I work mornings too.' Theo gulped down his cup of tea. 'Thanks for the drink, Cindy. I must be off now.'

*

Theo sat down at his desk. He could see Arthur staring out of his small window. This wasn't going to be easy; the old man's heart was already broken after the loss of his wife. Now the members of the parish council had ripped it in two. Theo could understand the need for the village to survive, but at the expense of Arthur? Now that was a tragedy.

There was a knock on Theo's door. 'Coooo-eeee, is our handsome village photographer in residence this morning?' Theo opened the door to the sight of Mrs Carruthers. 'There's a delivery for you downstairs, and you need to sign for it.' Mrs Carruthers' hazel eyes shone. It was such a delight having Theo around. Theo dashed down the stairs, and Mrs Carruthers peeped through the open doorway to his apartment, it wouldn't harm to have a little look inside.

On hearing the external door to the Post Office & General Store close, Mrs Carruthers crept back onto the upstairs landing and positioned her foot between the door of the apartment and the frame. 'I decided to guard your apartment for you. You didn't shut the door. Now that you're back I'll pop back downstairs and tell everyone what you're like . . . er, what you like . . . er, you know what I mean.'

Theo stared at his flustered landlady as she ran her hand through her short wiry grey hair. 'Are you feeling OK, Mrs Carruthers? You're sweating, and you're very flushed.' Mrs Carruthers just waved and ran down the stairs, out of the shop and into Cindy's Bakery.

'I don't know how to tell you, Cindy, and I'm not sure if it's good or bad.'

Cindy held a chair out for Mrs Carruthers to sit down and poured her a glass of water. Mrs Carruthers pulled out the chair beside her and ushered Cindy to sit down too. Pressing her hands to her pink cheeks, Mrs Carruthers continued: 'Our latest resident isn't just drop dead gorgeous, he knows it. He's a lothario. He's been sent here to become the heart of Truelove Hills in more ways than one. I'd bet my pension fund that Leticia Lovett has arranged it. She must be paying him a fortune to come down here from London and loaf around pretending he's a photographer until we get the swarm of tourists she's predicting and then he can do his "thing".'

Cindy took a gulp of water while Mrs Carruthers came up for air. 'Anyway, I must be off now, I've left the shop unattended, I just needed to confide in someone.' Mrs Carruthers dashed over the polished wooden floor with a spring in her step.

Cindy called after her. 'How did you find this out, Mrs Carruthers?'

'I've seen his signature. He's been practising it; lots of times. He just uses his initials "TT" and then draws a heart shape around them. Well, I ask you, what grown-up man does that sort of thing? He must be in his late twenties. He's practising his branding as . . . as some kind of gigolo! You just trust me, Cindy. Watch your step and don't do anything I wouldn't do.'

3

THE NAMING CEREMONY

It was Friday the 1st of March. How ironic; eighty years to the day Arthur Makepeace had named the village Pebblestown in a school competition. Arthur wasn't to be seen in the village square on this occasion. He'd become somewhat of a recluse over the past month.

Edgar Trueman took to the microphone: 'Testing, Tesssttting!!' The crowd gathered around the raised platform erected outside the Village Hall, and Lady Leticia Lovett scrambled onto the stage to stand beside Edgar. 'Today is the day our village comes to life. Pebblestown is no longer; from this point on we will be called TRUELOVE HILLS!'

There were cheers and a round of applause as Mrs Carruthers, an integral member of the village community, pulled a string to unveil the new village name on an elaborate wrought iron lamp-post outside the Village Hall.

Theo had been commissioned to take photographs of the momentous occasion, and he clicked away making sure he captured Lady Lovett's best side as she twisted and turned in a variety of poses. 'Now, Theo darling, I'm holding a drinks reception this evening at the chateau to which you are most cordially invited.'

Theo checked his watch and smiled brightly; it was five o'clock. 'I'm not sure if I can make it, I've promised to do a shoot of the talent competition at the Solent Sea Guest House in an hour.'

'Oh, darling, there are only three entrants. It'll all be over by six-thirty; plenty of time for you to arrive at the chateau by seven. I'll not take no for an answer; besides I have a little surprise and I want you to see it first.'

*

Lady Leticia had been correct; the talent competition was over in minutes. Only one contestant turned up; a beer-swigging yodeller who burped through his winning performance. An evening at the chateau didn't seem too bad after all. At seven o'clock precisely Theo pulled on the golden rope of a majestic door chime that hung to the right of two rustic wooden doors, forming the shape of an arch, to gain entrance into Chateau Amore de Pebblio.

The doors opened onto a pebbled courtyard with a cascading water feature on the far wall, Theo caught his breath. The magnificent fountain was illuminated to draw attention to the sculptures contained within it. A miniature version of Rome's Trevi Fountain sprang to mind. Theo shook his head; trust the Lady to live in such opulence.

A butler beckoned, and Theo followed him through a door to the left of the courtyard which led down a portrait adorned hallway opening up at the end into a large square room with black and white tiled floor, sweeping staircase and balconies. Lady Leticia waved from a balcony on the right before gliding along the landing and descending the stairs in a white lace dress complete with train. As soon as she stepped onto the tiled floor, a pianist began to play.

'Theo, my gorgeous man.' Leticia air-kissed Theo's crimson cheeks with her scarlet painted lips. 'I am so excited with how it's turned out. You wouldn't believe the mountains I've had to climb to make it happen. Of course, I've had to use my charm and intellect and all my other assets at once. But it's been well worth it, and I want you to be the first to sample the Truelove Hills experience.'

Theo took a step back feeling slightly out of his depth. The Lady was relentless in getting her way. She even had a miniature version of the Trevi Fountain in her courtyard, for goodness sake. This woman could have anything she wanted.

Leticia took hold of Theo's arm and led him out of the galleried chamber into a room a short way down a corridor on the right. It was dark, it smelled musty, and she put her hands over his eyes. 'Now, my darling, you are going to see something that will thrill you.' Leticia's hands fell to her sides as the lights turned on to reveal a small cinema room. Leticia picked up her train and took a seat in the middle of the front row. She gestured to Theo to sit next to her. The lights dimmed, the curtains opened, and the movie began . . . the movie of Truelove Hills.

It was a promotional advertisement for the tourism trade. It was quite good. There were overhead shots of the village, the hills, the pebblestone cottages and village square. The village green displayed loving couples sauntering around. The Lady must have hired actors for that bit. Of course, there was a big section on the accommodation available at Chateau Amore de Pebblio and a smaller account of the less expensive rooms at the Solent Sea fully-licensed Guest House. Cindy looked quite pretty shaking the red and white gingham tablecloth out of the door of her bakery and Mrs Carruthers didn't get to feature in the scene of the

Post Office & General Store. Theo grinned, Mrs Carruthers did look a bit formidable, maybe Lady Leticia had a facelift in mind for her in the near future.

All in all, Theo thought the Lady had done a good job – until – the very end. Leticia and Edgar appeared on the screen and announced: 'Trueman and Lovett combine to bring you Truelove Hills. This has been a production by Truelove Enterprises.'

Theo turned to face Leticia. 'You've changed the name of the village just to suit the two of you?'

Leticia clapped her hands with glee. 'Isn't it clever? Edgar and I practically own this place anyway what a better engagement present could any girl have? Edgar's asked me to marry him, and I've said "yes", we're a formidable force when we're together. When we marry we'll be changing our name to "Truelove", isn't that romantic? We have plans, there'll be no need for that guest house or bakery soon they're too downmarket for the clientele we intend attracting to our village; mine and Edgar's village. What do you think of my wedding dress, by the way? I needed to give it a whirl down those stairs ahead of the big day.'

Theo stood up in alarm. There must be something he could do to save the village from the clutches of these two disgusting characters. His mind was spinning. It was probably best to keep them onside for now until he had at least some idea of what to do.

4

WHEELS IN MOTION

Theo didn't get to sleep until four in the morning. He awoke with a start at seven. There was a banging noise downstairs which surprised him at such an early hour. Theo thought of the "big plans" for the village and wondered if the Post Office & General Store would survive the culling of Pebblestown memorabilia. The banging stopped and started up again over the road. Mrs Carruthers was struggling with an armful of flyers, nails between her teeth and a hammer in her hand. Theo pulled on his clothes and ventured outside to help her.

As he'd feared, Truelove Enterprises were moving full steam ahead with their undercover takeover bid of the village. The flyers were glossy advertisements aimed at attracting tourists to the area. Theo was even warming to the Truelove Hills concept that Edgar and Leticia had sold to the residents; he could see the potential in it. What he couldn't accept was the fact that the two of them were conniving and deceitful and powerful enough to effectively "own" a whole village that they'd named after themselves. Shocking, absolutely shocking.

Theo stared closer at the flyers. There was a photograph of him in the bottom right-hand corner under the heading: 'Theo Tressler Our Resident Photographer'. That was fine. What wasn't fine was the fact that a heart shape had been drawn around the photograph and the initials "TT" had been inserted at the bottom point of the heart.

Theo screwed up the leaflet and threw it in a bin. 'How could she do this? How could she turn me into a laughing-stock? Well, she's just about tested my patience now!'

Mrs Carruthers was startled by his outburst. 'What's the matter, Theo?'

'Leticia Lovett has tried to turn me into a love symbol, look at that heart around the photograph of me. How dare she do that?'

Mrs Carruthers held her hand to her chest and her knees buckled beneath her. Theo helped her sit down on a wall. 'It was my idea to do that.'

Theo raised his eyebrows. 'What on earth for?'

'I have to admit that I've seen your signature. You write your initials then draw a heart around them, I thought it would be a nice touch, and in keeping with the romantic mood we want to create for the village.'

Theo rubbed his forehead with both hands. This place was beyond belief. Mrs Carruthers had been into his room, and he was now being portrayed as some sort of heart-throb to attract people to Truelove Hills! Wait a minute – surely that gave him some power? Maybe this wasn't a bad thing after all. There must be some way he could turn the situation around to his advantage and ultimately save the village.

*

Firstly, Theo called in some favours from London. He knew of an investor, and he had to act quickly. There was a small parade of derelict shops in a side street that meandered up a hill opposite a boarded-up public house situated to the right of the Solent Sea Guest House. Edgar and Leticia had mentioned about knocking them down and building a four-storey carpark to cope with the influx of day trippers to the new Truelove Hills. Premium charges would apply of course. Theo had a vision for the shops. With their cobblestone facades they could become quaint again, and more visitors to the area would require more facilities resulting in more jobs for the locals.

Next, Theo needed to encourage Cindy to expand her bakery, or she wouldn't survive the takeover bid. A less easy conversation to have would be with David Makepeace. How could Theo influence a long-standing member of the community to try something different? What right did he have to move into the village and start coming up with ideas; ideas that would not be accepted by the parish council that was dominated by two repulsive characters? No, for some reason, Theo was not looking forward to speaking to David Makepeace in any shape or form. Indeed, he felt slightly nervous.

*

Cindy's long blonde hair was pulled back into a neat ponytail with a red and white gingham bow to match her apron and the tablecloths. She stared at the approaching figure of the village's future lothario through narrowed blue eyes and jumped as he pushed open the door to the bakery.

'Cindy, I'm so pleased you're on your own. I've a proposition I'd like to make to you. Please don't say "no" until you've heard me out. How would you like to expand your business to include a delicatessen and bistro?'

Cindy laughed, just a small laugh at first, then she pulled out a chair and sat down before the laughter turned into sobs and tears rolled down her cheeks.

Theo pulled out the chair next to her and leant towards her with his arms resting on his knees, and his hands open wide in surprise. 'I didn't mean to upset you. I thought the idea might excite you.'

Cindy took the handkerchief Theo was offering and blew her nose. 'I'm sorry, Theo, you just hit a raw nerve. I'm shocked at your suggestion. It's something I've always wanted but, apart from the fact I don't have the funds, I'm tied to the village. I'm very lucky to have one of the few jobs around here; I need to support my two younger brothers who can't get jobs anywhere near here. They'll leave for further afield before long, just like most of my generation. Pebblestown – sorry Truelove Hills – has lost its heart.'

Theo stood up and paced around the bakery collecting his thoughts. 'How old are your brothers, Cindy?'

Cindy's eyes widened. 'Nineteen and twenty.'

Theo nodded. 'That's good. Very good. It would be such a shame if the new Truelove Hills didn't have work for its residents wouldn't it?'

It was Cindy's turn to nod.

Theo headed towards the door. 'I'd appreciate it if you kept what we've just spoken about as a secret for now, I'm just fact-finding at the moment. To be honest with you, I have some reservations about the motives of Lady Lovett and Edgar Trueman with the village renaming and their plans for the future. It would take a better man than me to bring this village back to life in a way that benefits everyone, but I'm committed to helping.'

Theo was gone as quickly as he came, leaving Cindy in a whirlwind of thoughts. There was something about that man; he'd not been here five minutes, yet he fitted in so well. She felt she could trust him and he, indeed, had confided in her. Maybe Mrs Carruthers had uncovered something significant; maybe Theo Tressler had been sent to the village for a reason.

*

Theo strode through the front door of the Solent Sea fully-licensed Guest House with his shoulders back, and his head held high. David Makepeace was on the first-floor landing with a basket of replacement toiletries for the guest rooms. He called down the stairs: 'I'll be with you in a minute.'

David was surprised to see Theo shuffling his feet nervously in the entrance hall a few minutes later. His senses alerted him to "no good".

'David! I thought I'd pop by to see how things went after the talent contest.'

David Makepeace raised his bushy eyebrows and

scratched his curly head. That reminded him; he needed to take time for a haircut. His dad had said over a month ago that he looked like a shaggy sheep with too many unwieldy black curls for a man of fifty-four. Arthur Makepeace had always kept himself tidy even in his eighties, even after losing his Alice. David felt a lump in his throat, he missed talking to his dad, but the fallout at the parish council meeting in February meant that Arthur wasn't talking to anyone, he never left his cottage – or let anyone in.

David cleared his thoughts. 'I'm sorry – you mean the talent contest that never was. That yodeller sent the guests scurrying to their rooms by eight o'clock. As there were three rooms booked last night due to the day's shenanigans I decided to have an early night. I was up at the crack of dawn this morning. I don't usually need to take on help with breakfasts and the like until later in the year. This morning was an exception.'

Theo decided he had nothing to lose and took a deep breath. 'I was wondering why you don't take on the old public house next door. It would be a good fit with the guest house, and every village needs a good pub as a meeting place. It could turn out to be the centre of the community if it re-opened.'

David couldn't help but smile. Young men these days had no idea. No idea of how hard it was to run a business, keep afloat and just keep going with life when everything's against you. One business was enough for him, never mind two.

David was still smiling, but shaking his head too. He held the door to the guest house open and ushered Theo through it. Theo knew the conversation would be difficult; some people were just too set in their ways for their own good.

*

Arthur's cottage was next door to David's guest house. Arthur had ventured outside earlier that day. He was now sitting in his window holding one of the Truelove Hills flyers that had been so carefully erected by Mrs Carruthers.

There was an old shoebox at Arthur's feet. Alice had always put special things in there and, in the seven years since her passing, Arthur had continued the tradition. He'd worked out who Theo Tressler really was. There were no flies on Arthur.

5

PEBBLE PEAK

After a good night's sleep, Theo felt re-energised. There was so much work to do here, such a difference to make. Truelove Hills may truly be a hidden gem in the south of England; if it was developed with empathy and managed to its full potential. As usual, Theo drank his first coffee of the day and looked out of the window of his apartment over to Arthur Makepeace's cottage. This morning the daily delivery of groceries wasn't still on the doorstep at eight o'clock. Theo checked the lounge window directly opposite; there was no sign of Arthur.

Theo looked up the winding lane and then down to the village square to his right. There was still no sign of Arthur, but he must be OK, he had taken in his groceries earlier than usual. Theo felt comforted by that; he would keep an eye out for Arthur during the day.

After a quick shower, Theo grabbed his camera and pulled open his apartment door. There were no photo shoots booked, but he needed to look like he had a role to play in the community. Theo shut the door and locked it. His foot slid on a brown paper envelope on his doormat. Theo opened it and read the handwritten note:

To TT Loveheart. Bring your camera to Pebble Peak by nine this morning, and I'll teach you a thing or two. Arthur Makepeace.

Theo checked his watch; it was eight fifty-two. He ran down the stairs nearly knocking Mrs Carruthers over in the process. Holding her by the shoulders to steady her he gasped: 'Which way to Pebble Peak Mrs Carruthers?' Mrs Carruthers pointed up the lane and Theo ran as fast as he could.

Arthur's silver curls shone as he watched Theo running up the peak at the top of the lane and his silver moustache twitched in amusement. 'Not very good my boy, you're fifteen minutes late.'

Theo thought of arguing, but the moment passed. Arthur had a presence that left the younger man in awe.

'I am so sorry, Sir, about the renaming of the village. I know that it was very important for you to keep the name as Pebblestown, but I am starting to see some potential in the Truelove Hills branding.'

Arthur placed a hand on his heart, and his bright green eyes twinkled. 'Me too, my boy, me too.'

Theo was taken aback, why the sudden turnaround by this key member of the community? Arthur needed to know what Truelove Enterprises were planning. 'I know I can trust you, Sir. I've discovered that Lady Lovett and Edgar Trueman are planning a takeover of the village. Cindy's Bakery and your son's guest house won't be able to survive for long. Leticia and Edgar are even planning on getting married and changing their names to "Truelove". I'm dismayed at how far they've got with all of this. It is utterly wrong!'

Arthur smiled as he listened. 'You're not telling me anything I haven't figured out myself. No-one would listen to me mind – until you came along. I even have my own bit of "intelligence" that I've been keeping up my sleeve for when things get too close for comfort with those two gaining control.'

Theo was intrigued. 'What's that?'

'They won't be getting married or changing their names. Edgar Trueman is out to take Leticia Lovett for all she's worth. I've seen his plans for the redevelopment of that castle of hers and she doesn't feature in any part of it. Not even a mirror to show off her "best side" as she likes to put it. Everyone's been fooled except me.'

Theo sat down on the nearest large stone. 'What do you suggest we do?'

Arthur's eyes twinkled. 'I'm getting some thoughts. Now that you're the upcoming TT Loveheart you could play a key role and sweep her off her feet.'

Theo cringed at the thought. 'I really don't think I could deceive a Lady.'

Arthur was more matter of fact. 'It wouldn't take too much to woo her, and in the end, it would be for her own good. When she sees sense, she can really become part of the community. I can see that castle of hers playing a key role in what we should be achieving for the village. Are you up for it?'

Against his better judgement, Theo nodded.

'Now let me show you around Pebble Peak. How many peaks do you know of with a lake at the top?' Theo shook his head. 'Thought so. There are ducks too. I've been saying for many a year "it's all about the pebbles". I have a feeling that, finally, people may start to listen.'

*

There certainly was a lake, and ducks, and pebblestone buildings – basic and uninhabited. Theo's mind was racing, cheaper lodging up here than the Solent Sea, maybe a Glamping type of offering, with the chateau at the highest end of accommodation available in Truelove Hills.

This is amazing, Mr Makepeace. 'Why though do you keep saying: "It's all about the pebbles"?'

'Please call me Arthur. It's a very special story. I won the heart of my Alice through the pebbles. I came up here one day when I was fifteen years old and found a pebble in the shape of a heart. The letters "AA" were engraved on it, bit wobbly mind, me being a stonemason I should know. I kept the stone until I found a girl with an initial to match mine and that was my lovely Alice. We were married for over sixty years.'

Theo felt a warmness in his heart. 'That's an amazing story, Arthur.'

Arthur turned to face the lake. 'I want to bring what Alice and I had back to the village; happiness like no other. Of course, there were bad times; very bad indeed. We lost our beloved Harriet after she brought our four granddaughters into this world. I have a lot of time for David. He's been a good father to them all and Alice was a grandmother like no other, never a moment to herself with four wee lassies to look after.'

Theo's heart went out to the old man. He must be very lonely. 'Where are your granddaughters now, Arthur?'

'Well, Hannah's in Dubai, Matilda's in New York

and the youngest two, Tabitha and Tallulah are due home next month. They've nearly finished some sort of "arty" course in London. Do everything together those two; joined at the hip being twins. Not much chance of finding jobs for them here mind. Unless we come up with a cunning plan to get this whole Truelove Hills thing off the ground in a good way, not in the way that buffoon Edgar Trueman intends to pursue.'

6

A LADY TO WOO

With the imposing wooden arched doors before him, Theo breathed in before pulling on the golden rope. This time, Lady Leticia stood beside the butler to greet her guest, and Theo bowed as he handed her a bouquet of blue hyacinths, pink tulips and the palest yellow daffodils. Not an unusual array of flowers by any means, but even so, it had taken a taxi journey to the nearest town to buy them. Theo made a mental note that the village needed a florist.

'My dearest Theo, how very lovely. I was intrigued to receive your telephone call yesterday evening. It's only been two days since we last met. It's very convenient that my fiancé is currently on an aeroplane to America. We wouldn't want him getting jealous, now would we?'

Theo's mind was spinning; Edgar Trueman was out of the country – what a stroke of luck.

'I just wanted to return your hospitality, Lady Lovett. I am afraid that my apartment is quite insignificant compared to the chateau so I thought we could have lunch at Cindy's Bakery.'

The Lady sneezed then coughed, then sneezed again before throwing her bouquet in the air. 'I've never set foot in that establishment, and I certainly don't intend to.' The butler caught the flowers before they hit the pebblestone floor of the courtyard and Theo watched as Leticia's blonde bun-topped slender frame disappeared past the replica Trevi fountain and down the portrait adorned hallway.

The butler grinned at the young man's shocked expression. 'She's allergic to hyacinths. You'll have to try better than that.'

Theo took a step back and the chateau doors closed. In a way he felt quite relieved. The information he had gained about Edgar Trueman was worth the visit. An idea was coming to mind, a very bright one at that.

Arthur Makepeace had seen his new neighbour go out in a taxi and come back with flowers. He had watched him walk up the hill to woo the Lady. He hadn't expected him to be walking down the hill again so soon, without the flowers and on his own. Arthur moved briskly to his front door and opened it just as Theo was about to knock.

'Come in, my boy. Tell me what happened.'

'Lady Leticia's allergic to hyacinths. She won't set foot inside Cindy's Bakery, and Edgar Trueman's on his way to America.'

Both men burst into laughter. 'Well, you had a close shave there, son. You got some good intelligence though. It's time for us to make our next move. From what you tell me, Cindy will be onside with our coup. We can easily overthrow Edgar; particularly with him being out of the country and from what I know about his dodgy dealings, when we've done that, Leticia will fall in line. The Lady won't want her castle turning into a casino.'

Theo raised his eyebrows. 'Casino?'

'Yes. That's his plan. If that oaf has his way, he'll turn our village into Las Vegas.'

Arthur rubbed his forehead. 'There's only one stumbling block at the moment, and that's my David. He needs to apologise to me. He should come grovelling, cap in hand. I'd have preferred him to have done that himself, but you'll need to give him a push. You can perhaps give him the heads up about the casino. He won't like that idea.'

Theo noticed the sadness in Arthur's eyes and instinctively gave him a hug. 'Don't worry Arthur. I'll pop in to see David before I go to see Cindy, she's pulled out all the stops to make lunch for my big date that never was. Once David has apologised bring him over to the bakery, and we can have our own Extraordinary Meeting of the parish council. The tables have turned, Arthur, there will be four of us now on the right side, not the wrong one, and soon we'll have Lady Leticia joining us too.

Arthur closed the door after Theo's exit. He sat down at his writing bureau and wrote a note addressed to Lady Leticia. The postman stopped cycling on his weary climb up the pebblestone hill when he heard Arthur's whistle. He hadn't been stopped in his tracks by Arthur for a long time. He left his bike on the pavement and walked down to the envelope-waving old man.

'Drop this in at that castle up there, would you? There's a good man.'

The postman saluted. 'Yes, Sir.' It was good to have the old Arthur back. He hadn't whistled since Alice died.

*

Cindy watched the surprising events through the

bakery window. Theo without the Lady; Theo going into Arthur's and then the Solent Sea Guest House; Arthur summoning the postman; David rushing out of his door and into his father's cottage; Theo now heading towards the bakery . . .

'Cindy, I have some excellent news. Things are coming together at a pace. Wow, sausage rolls, pasties, cakes and sandwiches too!'

Theo grabbed a sausage roll, sat down and began to relay the extraordinary chain of events to a giggling and excited Cindy. Within fifteen minutes they were joined by Arthur and David. Lady Leticia arrived by chauffeur-driven car thirty minutes after that to take her first ever well-heeled step into Cindy's Bakery. A plan was coming together.

Everyone stood to acknowledge the Lady's entrance, and Arthur held out a chair. Leticia perched on the edge of it before airing her frustrations. 'A casino! How could he do that to me? He said we were powerful and that together we would own Truelove Hills. I had absolutely no idea that he was planning to turn Chateau Amore de Pebblio into a casino!'

Cindy pushed a plate of scones in front of the Lady, and she proceeded to plaster one with cream and jam before taking a large mouthful.

Theo turned on his charm. 'It is quite clear to us,

Lady Lovett, that you are the most powerful person in the village. You are even more powerful on your own without Edgar Trueman trying to turn your undoubted success to his advantage.'

The Lady kicked off her shoes and reached for a sausage roll. 'Well just between us, Edgar has passed Chairmanship of the parish council over to me while he's away. I'm officially in charge for the next month.'

Arthur patted David on the arm. 'I think this calls for champagne. Pop back over the road and find us your largest bottle.'

7

RETURN OF THE TWINS

Tabitha and Tallulah Makepeace: A double whirlwind if ever there was one. Full of energy and opinions except when it came to themselves. Between them, they had not one idea of where their future lay, except that it had to be together. With their long curly red hair, emerald green eyes and freckles they were a force to be reckoned with, even more so being identical.

Tallulah knocked on Arthur's door, and Tabitha held the box. It was a big box tied with a large red ribbon.

Arthur had seen them through the window. 'Come on in you two, since when did you decide to knock?'

Tallulah dashed in and hugged her grandfather. 'Oh Grandpa, it's sooooo good to see you! We've brought you a surprise from London.' She took hold of the box from Tabitha so that she too could hug Arthur.

Arthur raised a bushy silver eyebrow. 'What's in the box?'

The girls looked at each other and grinned before placing the box on the floor and screeching in unison: 'Open it up and see!!!'

As soon as Arthur untied the red ribbon the lid moved. It moved around until it fell off, revealing what was inside – a small white fluffy dog.

'What on earth have you done this time? You know your father won't let you have a dog.'

Tabitha picked the dog up and stroked its hair-emitting fur while it licked her face. Tallulah did the talking. 'He's called "Fluffy". We don't know what type he is except that he's a mixture. He's had all his vaccinations, and we've got a basket for him and some food. He's all yours, Grandpa. We've bought him for you to keep you company.'

Arthur stood up from his window seat. 'I am saying this now and saying it only once. You will need to take the dog back. They shouldn't be selling pets to young girls who should know better.'

Tabitha thrust Fluffy into Arthur's arms. 'Grandpa, we're 21. Like it or not we're not young girls any more. We're young women with minds of our own. We need to go and say hello to Daddy now. We'll be back soon to check on you both.'

The twins kissed Fluffy then Arthur and made a quick exit.

Fluffy licked Arthur's hand, and Arthur put him down on the floor. How long were those girls going to leave them alone? He didn't know how to look after a dog. All he knew was that they drank water and ate dog biscuits. He went into the kitchen to find a shallow bowl and a biscuit. It was cold in the kitchen. His living room was nice and warm with the fire going. It was best to keep Fluffy in the same room so he could keep his eye on him until the twins came back. The dog appeared to smile up at Arthur at the sight of the biscuit, and the old man's heart began to melt. Within no time at all Fluffy was asleep by the fire and when the girls returned with dog basket and provisions their mission had been accomplished. Their grandfather was alone no more.

*

The return of the twins meant that two of the Solent Sea's six guest rooms were out of action. David Makepeace had his own one-bedroom private apartment in the building, but with the summer season around the corner and all the new plans that Theo chap was coming up with, David was concerned that he'd start losing out on revenue. Maybe taking on the public house next door wasn't such a bad idea. There was accommodation above it which would help with the shortage of bedrooms, and there would be work for the girls. Another idea sprang to mind; Cindy Copperfield's brothers. David had always kept an eye out for Cindy after her parents retired to Spain. She was a good friend of his daughter Matilda's. The two young lads could help the twins with any heavy lifting, and if they were any good in the kitchen, then they could help David with the guest house breakfasts too. Yes, he could see it now: David Makepeace, proprietor of the Solent Sea fully-licensed Guest House and the village Public House. The pub needed a name; it needed a name . . .

*

Tabitha and Tallulah were chatting with Mrs Carruthers when a van arrived from London. It parked outside the Post Office & General Store and the driver offloaded four large boxes that required a signature. Mrs Carruthers signed for them; they were addressed to Theo.

Mrs Carruthers had known the twins all their lives. They had been mischievous and annoying in their youth, but they seemed to be maturing well now. They were even keen to pay attention to a bit of gossip here and there that Mrs Carruthers had managed to uncover. 'Now girls, I have no idea what's in these boxes for the village heart-throb.' Mrs Carruthers raised her eyes to the ceiling. 'He lives up there you know. He says he's a photographer, but I have my doubts. What do we need with a photographer in our small village?'

The door to the Post Office & General Store flew open, and Theo unravelled his scarf before combing his hair with his fingers. 'It's blowing a gale out there, Mrs Carruthers. I've just spoken to the delivery driver. Thank you for signing for these boxes. I'll take them upstairs out of your way.' Theo flashed a dimpled smile at the twins and proceeded to lift one of the boxes.

The girls pounced on a box each. Tabitha made the introductions. 'Let us help you. We're Tabitha and Tallulah Makepeace, and we've heard all about you.'

Theo's smile faded. How much had they heard about him? He felt disconcertingly uncomfortable in their presence. Things were going so well until now.

Once the twins had left, Theo made a phone call to thank his friend in London for forwarding on his belongings.

'Thanks for sending on my things, Jamie. I had no idea how this was going to all pan out. It's taking off now at a pace, and I need your support. Can you take some time off and come down here at short notice? I'd really appreciate it, bud. See you soon.'

*

Tabitha and Tallulah sat on a bench at the edge of the village green reflecting. Things had changed since they went away to London three years ago: Grandpa seemed happier; Daddy was more open to change; Mrs Carruthers had a twinkle in her eye and that was only what they'd noticed in the first couple of days back.

'Do you mind if we sit with you?'

The girls jumped out of their thoughts to find Cindy Copperfield's two annoying brothers, Steve and Bruce, standing over them.

Tallulah made the decision. 'No thanks.'

Steve's light blue eyes opened widely at the remark, and Bruce's narrowed, a glimmer of brooding sapphire just visible. The men turned their backs and wandered back to the village square. They were both blonde, the same as Cindy. Steve was renowned to have fewer haircuts than this brother, and his shoulder-length curls were in stark contrast to Bruce's short back and sides with quiff at the front.

Tabitha's eyes were on stalks. 'Since when did *they* grow up?'

8

BACK TO WORK

Arthur's back garden was long and narrow, the same width as his cottage and the depth of the Solent Sea Guest House next door. Arthur whistled as he rummaged through the top drawer of his writing bureau. Where were they? They hadn't seen the light of day for at least ten years. Fluffy scampered around at his feet sensing the excitement.

'Here they are, Fluffy!' Arthur held a set of keys aloft, and winked at the dog before marching through the kitchen and opening his back door. Fluffy's tail wagged as the pair breathed in the fresh spring air on the short trip to the fence at the end of Arthur's plot of land.

Arthur bent down to pick up Fluffy and the dog peered over the fence with his master. 'Now, you see that shed over there? It's mine. I bought the bit of land it's on many years ago so that I could run my business just a stone's throw from home. I never wanted to be too far from Alice and,' Arthur put Fluffy down before inserting a key into a rusty padlock and opening a gate in the fence, 'this was the perfect solution.'

The shed was large, dusty and covered in cobwebs; yet it was tidy. A workbench in the middle of the room was laden with a variety of tools all lined up in size order. Arthur's hand ran over them. 'We won't need all of these for what we'll be doing. Just a small chisel and mallet will do us nicely.'

*

With Lady Leticia temporarily in charge of the parish council, there was no time to waste. The committee unanimously approved the following plans during a hastily scheduled meeting hosted by David Makepeace in the lounge bar of the empty public house:

Chateau Amore de Pebblio
High-class accommodation, à la carte restaurant, wedding venue, conference facilities. Ready now. Advertise immediately.

Public House
David Makepeace to take over proprietorship. In need of renovation. Enlist the help of Makepeace twins and Copperfield brothers.

Theo Tressler to secure funding. Scheduled opening 1 July.

Cindy's Bakery, Delicatessen and Bistro
Cindy's Bakery to move to small parade of derelict shops to make room for delicatessen and bistro. Advertise job opportunities for local staff. Theo Tressler to secure funding. Scheduled opening 1 July.

Glamping Accommodation at Pebble Peak
Arthur Makepeace to supervise. Theo Tressler to secure funding. Scheduled opening 1 June.

Lady Leticia sat back in her chair. 'Well, I must say, everyone, we've made more progress at one meeting than in the past decade. If you meet your deadlines, we'll be fully open for business in the summer.'

David Makepeace was less than enthused. 'We're taking on too much at once. Also, I'll believe all this funding that's supposed to be coming when I see it.' David flashed a sideways glance at Theo then raised his eyes.

Arthur came to Theo's defence. 'Give the lad a chance. He's got no reason to come here and mess with us. If anything, he's helped save us all from the clutches of Edgar Trueman.'

Lady Leticia blushed before rising from her chair.

'Well, if that's all for now, I consider this meeting closed. I'll arrange the promotional material. As the chateau is already fully operational, I er . . . I could help out if so required with any of the other ventures, only if absolutely necessary of course.'

Theo turned his mobile on as soon as the Lady left the room. He had seven missed calls – all from Jamie. He made his excuses and hurried back to his apartment.

*

Arthur liked it when a plan came together; he hadn't had so much fun in years. If the Lady was ready to take guests at the chateau, then he needed to start his business going straight away. He opened the door to his cottage to be greeted by a bouncing and yapping Fluffy. There was a hessian sack behind the front door and Arthur grabbed it before reaching for a packet of dog treats on the sideboard. 'Come on, Fluffy; we're going to Pebble Peak. We'll pass a castle on the hill on the left. I need you to remember where it is.'

Fluffy didn't need a lead; there wasn't any traffic. Dog and master climbed the hill that led from the High Street to Pebble Peak. There was a mansion on the left and Arthur stopped outside the arched wooden gates. 'This is the castle, Fluffy.' Fluffy cocked his leg up the wooden door frame. 'Good boy! Now off we go to Pebble Peak.'

*

Theo punched the air. Tomorrow! Jamie was coming tomorrow! He rubbed his hands together then fell back on his bed. How had things escalated this far – this fast? It was only the last week in April. He hadn't been planning on bringing a whole village back to life. He'd only wanted to get to know one or two people. Somehow though, he'd become part of the community, and it felt good, really good.

*

Arthur sat on a large stone by the lake, those buildings that Theo had in mind for Glamping were sturdy enough. Arthur should know; he'd helped build them as a boy. There were just four of them; one for each season. It was a school project back in the day to build a summer-house, and it turned out to be so popular that the children in the community decided to build an autumn-house, a winter-house and a spring-house too. Arthur sighed. There was no school in the village now – no need for one with no children.

Arthur reached down and picked up a pebble the size of his palm. Fluffy sat at his feet watching. 'Now come along, Fluffy, I need a bit of help. My back and knees aren't too good for bending these days. See the size of this pebble? I need you to find me some more. Off you go now boy; there's a good dog.'

The sack was heavy on the way back to the shed, Arthur was grateful the journey was downhill. He had to keep stopping to rest, and Fluffy cocked his leg at every opportunity. Arthur smiled; that dog would never get lost, he'd well and truly marked his way home.

9

ANOTHER NEWCOMER

Mrs Carruthers held the man's hand in both of hers. It was her way of giving the most welcoming handshake she could think of. His hand was smooth and tanned with manicured nails. In fact, the whole of him was tanned, his dark blonde hair was bleached by the sun, and his long eyelashes framed his turquoise eyes to perfection.

After taking a long sniff of expensive aftershave and releasing his hand, Mrs Carruthers was lost for words, so she said the first thing that sprang to mind: 'Have you been on holiday?'

Jamie smiled down at her. He was tall too, well over six feet. 'I wish, Mrs Carruthers. Just one of many business trips I'm afraid. The last one took six weeks to close a deal. I'm pleased to be back on this side of the world again, for the time being at least. There's no better place to be than England in the spring.'

'What did you say your name was again?'

'Jamie.'

'Jamie what? Just in case you get any post.'

'Just Jamie and I won't be getting any post while I'm in Truelove Hills.'

Mrs Carruthers raised an eyebrow. There was something not quite right about Jamie.

Theo ran down the stairs to greet his friend. 'Jamie! It's so good to see you. It's been way too long.'

Mrs Carruthers watched as the men embraced each other. Theo seemed a bit too keen to usher Jamie up to his apartment, and she heard them whispering as they charged up the stairs. Something was going on, she just knew it.

Jamie looked out of the apartment window. 'So that's Arthur's house directly opposite, with the Solent Sea on the right and the pub on the right of that. Did you say the chateau was up the hill on the left and Pebble Peak is at the top? I can see why you've identified investment opportunities for this place. It's a hidden gem.'

Theo scratched his head. 'You know why I came

here, Jamie. Money making wasn't my plan. I have to admit I feel uncomfortable with how things are turning out. I've just kind of got on a rollercoaster, and I can't get off.'

Jamie slapped Theo on the back. 'Well, leave the funding side of things to me. Papa will buy into your plans I'm sure. Now, where did you say I'll be staying for the next few days?'

'I thought you could sample the accommodation at the chateau and assess whether it's as good as Lady Leticia claims it is. She's got her first guests arriving next week from New York.'

'That's impressive. She must be paying her PR company a fortune.'

'Talking about that; I'm concerned about how much Edgar Trueman has already invested in the "Truelove Hills" image. We know he's a con man, who didn't have the interests of the community at heart, but he'll be back before long, and then all hell will break loose.'

'Don't worry about this Trueman guy, he's completely outnumbered. There will be other buildings, in numerous other places, that he can turn into casinos. Papa will pay him off if necessary.'

Theo exhaled deeply. 'Phew! It's so good to have you here.'

*

'My word, Lady Lovett, that's a replica of the Trevi Fountain in Rome. How on earth did you think of building that in your courtyard?'

The Lady held her arms out wide and did a twirl. 'I have lots of ideas, Jamie, and lots of money to help me put them into action.'

Jamie frowned. 'Did Edgar Trueman pay anything towards the "Truelove Hills" branding? Has he provided any funding at all?'

Leticia's eyes clouded over. 'Well, no. It's only now I realise he didn't love me. He just wanted my money to turn Chateau Amore de Pebblio into a casino!' The Lady let out a wail, and Jamie stepped towards her holding her shoulders in both hands.

'Now look at me. You don't need Edgar Trueman, you never did. You're a strong independent woman and much more powerful on your own. Will you do something for me?' Leticia nodded. 'Call Edgar Trueman when he wakes up later today,' Jamie looked at his watch, 'with the time difference a call through to him in about two hours should do it, and tell him never to come back. Break it off with him before he breaks things off with you. You owe him nothing; Truelove Hills owes him nothing. Get in there first and let him go off and find another rich woman to deceive.'

*

Jamie ran his hand over the ottoman at the end of the four-poster bed. The chateau reminded him of home. It was indeed impressive, and Lady Leticia had advised him that she was doubling her staff to cope with the anticipated influx of guests.

Theo had hit on a gold mine here. It was crucial though that the village didn't lose its charm. The pebblestone High Street that climbed up past the chateau to Pebble Peak needed to be pedestrianised. There was plenty of room for parking on the outskirts of the village. There would never be far to walk for anyone to get to the village centre. Cindy's new business would be up a side street opposite the public house and not far from her current premises. Now there was a thought. There would be an empty shop once the bakery had relocated. Jamie needed to call Theo with an update, so he'd mention the shop at the same time.

'Theo, it's Jamie. The chateau is in fine form, and Lady Leticia is upscaling on the staff front so service levels shouldn't dip. I've uncovered the fact that Edgar Trueman was just after the poor woman's money; he's not funded anything himself. The village owes him nothing. Once the Lady cuts her ties with him, he'll scarper. Oh, just one more thing, the bakery opposite the Solent Sea, don't know if you've got any plans for that once the shop becomes vacant.'

Theo closed his eyes and crossed his fingers. 'I have an idea for the empty shop. Just leave that to me.'

10

GLAMPING FOR ALL SEASONS

Arthur had become accustomed to sitting on a large stone by the lake while he supervised the work on the Glamping site. It was May now and, after the brief visit by Theo's friend Jamie, things had taken off. Builders of all kinds had descended on the village, and there was no shortage of skill sets or resources.

Leticia was playing an active part in all of the renovations. Today she was spending time with Arthur and Fluffy at Pebble Peak. Arthur couldn't resist a chuckle. Never in his lifetime had he seen the Lady wearing denim dungarees with her blonde hair covered by a floral scarf. Bright yellow rubber gloves were an essential accessory to her outfit along with white pumps which were looking shabbier by the day.

'What time are your guests from New York arriving?'

Leticia rolled back a rubber glove to check her watch. 'Good question, Arthur. In two hours. I need to get back to the chateau in preparation. By the way, I've been meaning to say that I like the idea of naming the Glamping huts after the four seasons. I believe it would add to the effect for the interior designs to reflect the names. Just a thought, your project though.'

Arthur watched the Lady skip back down the hill. Something had changed in her, and he couldn't quite put his finger on it. She'd had a good idea about the huts though. Arthur reached inside his jacket pocket for a pen and paper. Note written, he held out his hand to Fluffy and showed him a doggie treat. 'Here's one now and there'll be another for when you get back. Take this to the twins. Off you go now; there's a good dog.'

Fluffy returned twenty minutes later with a different note, his tail wagging. Arthur handed him his treat. 'What's this, Fluffy? I sent a note to ask the twins to come up here. I thought they'd come back with you.'

Arthur read the note: *'We're busy at the moment, Grandpa. We'll be with you in around an hour or so. Love T & T xx'*

Arthur sighed, he'd had a good idea he knew the

twins would like. Still, it would keep. He had to keep the work moving, and he wandered over to speak to the builders who were on a tea break.

'That shower block's coming along nicely. I wasn't sure at first that it would be in keeping with the huts.' Arthur shook his head and smiled. 'It's taken a bit of time for me to get used to the houses being called "huts". I can see the point though "Glamping huts" works well. We only planned to build one summerhouse when I was a boy, and we ended up building one for each season. Funny how things turn out. Best to move with the times though that's what I always say.'

The builders liked chatting with Arthur; it was the highlight of their day. He was so interesting and he'd offered them a discount if they returned with their families to spend their holidays in Truelove Hills. 'Bring the children!' he'd say.

There was a kerfuffle in the distance, and the builders turned their heads to look.

'Grandpa! We've got a surprise for you.'

The twins were standing either side of a person covered in a white sheet.

Arthur's eyes twinkled at the sight, and he suppressed a chuckle. 'Don't tell me – you've captured a ghost.'

'Better than that, Grandpa.'

The sheet was pulled off to reveal . . .

Arthur held his hand to his heart. 'Matilda! My little Tilly. When did you get back from New York? We weren't expecting you.'

Matilda hugged her grandfather. 'I've only just got back. I managed to persuade my boss and his assistant to come here for a couple of days before we go London for a conference. They're really impressed with the chateau. We've just taken them there on our way up to see you.'

Arthur frowned. 'So Leticia's only got guests because you brought them here?'

Matilda tied her waist-length wavy brown hair into a ponytail. 'Is that a problem Grandpa?'

Arthur could see the concern in his granddaughter's large blue eyes. 'No problem at all my lovely. No problem at all.'

Fluffy ran circles around Matilda's ankles. 'You must be Fluffy. The girls have told me all about you.'

Tallulah linked her arm through Arthur's. 'What did you want to see us for, Grandpa? It must be important to summon us up to Pebble Peak.'

Arthur coughed. 'Well, I've decided to name the

Glamping thingies "Spring", "Summer", "Autumn" and "Winter". Leticia thought it would be a good idea to deck them out inside to match their names. I then had another thought; with your arty skills can you paint the outsides to match the names? It has to be tasteful mind, none of that graffiti stuff.'

The twins squealed in unison. 'Of course, we can!'

Matilda cradled Fluffy in her arms and stroked his fur. Something had changed since she'd left home and it wasn't just the name of the village or the planned renovations; Truelove Hills was developing a heart.

'Coo-eeee, Arthur!' Everyone turned to witness Lady Lovett tottering up the hill with her American guests. 'I would like you to meet Mr Freemont and Miss Halliday.'

The couple shook hands with everyone on the top of Pebble Peak. Arthur scrutinised them. So these were the type of people Matilda worked with: Polished, professional, perfect. On initial inspection, Arthur couldn't find fault with either of them. That was a shame; Matilda wouldn't come home if she was surrounded by nice people. She was a good girl, Matilda, not a bad word to say about anyone. Arthur rubbed his chin. Truelove Hills needed Matilda more than New York did. He's always known that, but he'd never be the one to clip her wings.

11

RUMOURS OF A ROMANCE

Mrs Carruthers flung open the door to Cindy's Bakery and scanned the room. 'Is there anyone about, Cindy, or is it just the two of us?'

Cindy wiped her hands on her apron. 'It's just us, Mrs Carruthers.'

'Good. Leticia Lovett has just been in the shop and advised me that those two Americans have checked in at the chateau under different names and they've booked single rooms.'

'Well, that makes sense.'

'No, it doesn't. To travel all the way over here together and book into the same place is suspicious to me.'

'Trust me, Mrs Carruthers, it's perfectly normal these days for people to travel on business together and stay under the same roof. I'm surprised you're even questioning it. Anyway, Matilda tells me her boss is happily married and that his assistant has a fiancé. Nothing's going on between those two.'

Having no luck with Cindy, Mrs Carruthers popped over the road to see Arthur. 'I can feel it in my water, Arthur. Matilda's boss has eyes for his assistant; it's written all over his face.'

Arthur frowned. Matilda wouldn't like that rumour to be true now, would she? 'Leave it with me. I'll get to the bottom of what's going on.'

Arthur stepped out of his cottage and headed for the Solent Sea Guest House. Matilda was staying there with her father and the twins. He popped his head around the private lounge door. 'Just a quick one, Tilly. What are the names of your boss and his assistant?'

Matilda turned around in surprise. 'You must remember, Grandpa. It's Mr Freemont and Miss Halliday.'

Arthur waved an arm in the air. 'Of course, I know that; I'm not losing my memory yet. What do *you* call the pair of them?'

'Ross and Flick.'

'Flick?'

'It's short for Felicity.'

Arthur turned on his heels. 'Thanks. That's all I needed to know.'

*

Arthur had already done a deal with the butler at the chateau. When Fluffy barked outside the wooden arched gates, the butler needed to read Arthur's note, take the object from the bag attached to the dog's collar and follow the instructions. There would be a pint of the finest ale provided free of charge the next time the butler frequented the Solent Sea fully licensed Guest House.

*

Matilda jumped up from the sofa. 'Is that the time? I'm meeting my colleagues at the chateau in less than twenty minutes. I shouldn't be long. I'm doing a speech at the conference in London, and they want to hear it in advance. I'm petrified; I hate public speaking it was hard enough having to stand up in front of the class at school for "show and tell". It's just not me. I'd rather take a back seat.'

David Makepeace stared at his kind, loving daughter. What on earth was she doing living in New York and making speeches in London? It didn't suit her. He was still flummoxed about why she went to America in the first place, it just happened all of a sudden and was entirely out of character.

*

Matilda stood by the piano in the grand hallway of the chateau. She couldn't resist pressing a couple of keys as she waited for Ross and Flick to come down from their rooms. Matilda had always wanted to play the piano, but she'd never taken the time to learn. Any spare time she had was given to writing. She'd always written stories from a very young age; her head was in the clouds most of the time. It was pure luck that the Literary Agency in London she was working for had a vacancy in New York at the time when she most needed to get away. She didn't mind her job most of the time but being thrown into the spotlight was something she was struggling to accept. At least her boss was lovely, and Flick had become a good friend.

First, there was a scream, raised voices then the slamming of doors. Matilda moved to the bottom of the stairs and stared up at the balcony. After five minutes another door slammed, and Flick came into sight dragging her case.

'You dirty, cheating, scoundrel!!! You can keep your measly job. I've been headhunted by Flox and Co anyway. I was going to tell you when we got back to New York, but after what you've just done, I won't be spending another minute in your company. You'd better pay me my notice period or your wife will get to hear about this!'

Flick pushed past Matilda. 'Don't, whatever you do, trust that man. He's vile. Can you believe that I thought butter wouldn't melt in his mouth; that he was good, clean, wholesome and happily married? Well, not a word of it is true. Stay away from him, Matilda, while you still have your dignity intact.'

Matilda froze on the spot, her hand to her mouth. What had just happened? The butler ran down the road to Arthur's cottage. 'You'd better come quick and take your granddaughter home; she's in shock. I don't think she'll be going anywhere again soon.'

*

Matilda sat in Arthur's chair in the window of his cottage. She clasped both hands around the mug of hot chocolate her grandfather had made for her. Her world had collapsed yet again. She didn't want to go back to New York, and she definitely couldn't go back to London.

It was getting dark now, and Arthur turned on a lamp before putting another log on the fire. He looked out of the window and across the street. Everything was as it should be. There was no time better than this.

'Do you remember when you came home from

London to visit last year, and you sat at my bureau to write one of those stories of yours?'

Matilda's eyes widened, and she nodded.

'Well, you did a lot of doodling at the time.' Arthur lifted the lid of Alice's old shoebox and gave Matilda a piece of paper. 'I found this after you left and I didn't like to throw it away, so I put it in your grandmother's special box. You see, I thought it must be special with all those hearts on it.'

Tears flowed down Matilda's cheeks. She had drawn hearts, hearts with two "T"s inside. There was a scribble at the bottom of the page: *'Must return Theo's call.'*

'Theo's quite an unusual name isn't it?'

Matilda took Arthur's handkerchief and nodded again.

'Is that him up there in the window above Mrs Carruthers' store?' Arthur turned Matilda to face the window. 'Tilly and Theo – got a nice ring to it. He's a good boy; he's got my approval. Now, why hasn't he got yours?'

Matilda burst into tears and ran into the kitchen. Arthur followed her. 'I made a mistake, Grandpa. I got it wrong, and when I realised, there was no going back. It was Theo that was meant to go to New York; he's a stockbroker. He was offered a secondment for six months and I wouldn't let him take it. He wanted to go because he was promised a partnership in his firm when he came back to London. I was selfish and jealous, and I ended things because I was certain he thought more of his job than he did of me. He turned the secondment down, but I was too stubborn to admit I was wrong and, even worse, I took a job in New York instead, which made it look like I put my career ahead of him. It's such a mess, Grandpa. He'll never forgive me.'

Arthur put his arm around his granddaughter. 'I'd say he's pulled out all the stops to win you back. Why's he not in London now? Why is he bringing the heart back to our village? He's doing it all for you, Tilly. Now go over the road and make it up to him. Oh, but before you go, I need to pop out to the shed.'

Arthur returned with a heart-shaped pebble engraved with two "T's". I made this for you. I've been making a few pebble hearts recently. I've got a little supply now for when I need to engrave them.

Matilda ran over the road just as the butler knocked on Arthur's door. 'Any chance of that pint now? I did as you instructed and put that pebble on that woman's bed. Who'd have thought it would have caused such a commotion?'

12

IT'S ALL ABOUT THE PEBBLES

Theo ran down the stairs and opened the door to the Post Office & General Store before Matilda could reach it. 'Tilly! I can't believe you're here.' Theo reached out to embrace her, but Matilda folded her arms and scowled at him.

'What do you think you're playing at? You ruined my life in London, and now you've turned up in my home village, charmed everyone who matters to me and just taken over like you own the place. We don't need stockbrokers in Pebblestown.'

Theo flashed a smile that made Tilly's knees tremble. 'Don't forget about the name change; we're in Truelove Hills now. So much is changing, Tilly, even your grandfather approves. There's so much potential here for development, Jamie's been here to have a look around. His father's keen to become an investor so that we can get all of our projects off the ground. I have so much work to do here at the moment, and enough money saved so that I don't need to return to London just yet. They're holding my job open for me though in case things don't work out here.'

Matilda unfolded her arms and raised her eyebrows. 'Jamie. Jamie Thistlewaite? We need to discuss this in private.' Theo followed Matilda as she headed up the stairs to his apartment and Mrs Carruthers stood up from her crouching position behind the Post Office counter. Jamie Thistlewaite – now that put a whole different slant on things.

*

Arthur carried the basket by its handle. He'd draped a tea towel over the top to hide the contents, and he whistled as he entered his son's private apartment at the Solent Sea Guest House. 'Where are the twins?'

David Makepeace peered over the top of his newspaper. 'They're in their rooms, said they were doing some sketches for painting the Glamping huts or something. Full of ideas those two.'

Arthur reached into his pocket and produced a dog treat. 'Here you go, Fluffy. One now and another when you come back down the stairs. Go up there and bark as loud as you can. Those girls will come running when they hear you.'

Two minutes later and Arthur had the audience he

wanted. 'Matilda won't be going back to New York, so you'd best make up another guest room for her. Three of your girls are home now, David, and there's every chance they'll be around for a while longer.' Arthur winked at Tabitha and Tallulah.

Tallulah grinned as she stood with hands on hips. 'Grandpa, what have you done?'

Arthur stroked his silver moustache. 'It's all about the pebbles. Always has been, always will be.' With a flick of his wrist, Arthur removed the tea towel to reveal a basket full of heart-shaped pebbles. 'Voila!'

Tabitha picked one up to feel its smoothness and marvel at the craftsmanship. 'Didn't you say, Grandpa, that you once found a heart-shaped pebble up at Pebble Peak with the initials "AA" on it? That's when you realised that Grandma was the one for you?'

Arthur's eyes twinkled. 'Well, sometimes the pebbles need a little bit of help. I made one of these and left it where I knew your grandmother would sit to feed the ducks on the lake. She was craftier than me though. She engraved it with two "A's" and put it back for me to find. I never told anyone until this day that I made the heart in the first place; even my Alice. And, Alice never knew that I'd worked out she'd done the engraving. Love works in mysterious ways, it just sometimes needs a bit of help to get things going.'

It was David Makepeace's turn to comment. 'So, what do you intend doing with all the hearts you've made? Don't tell me you're trying to find another woman?'

Arthur shifted from one foot to another. 'One woman was enough for me. No one will replace my Alice. I'm just going to help things along when I see an opportunity. I've used two of the hearts already with outstanding results. You could say I've got a 100% success rate.'

The twins clapped their hands and squealed as they danced around the room. Their grandfather always had a way of making things happen. He'd lost his way a bit after losing his Alice, but his spirit was back now and if there was one person who could be relied upon to do the best thing for Truelove Hills it was him.

*

Mrs Carruthers tapped away on the keyboard of her computer. The internet was her speciality. There! There he was: *'Jamie Thistlewaite, London stockbroker convicted of corporate fraud.'*

Shaking her head, Mrs Carruthers jumped off her chair behind the Post Office counter and trotted off down the aisle of the General Store to fetch a packet of chocolate biscuits. Back on her chair, she had a better read of the online article. There was a picture of him; the gutless rogue shielded his face with an arm and was wearing a hoodie. What a liar! He'd told her that he'd been on the other side of the world, not in prison. Mrs Carruthers decided to do a more thorough check just to be sure. No – there was only one Jamie Thistlewaite in the world as far as she could see. No wonder he didn't want to divulge his surname. Mrs Carruthers had acquired highly sensitive information and she didn't know what to do. If she exposed him, the village would lose its funding, its future and its heart . . .

*

Theo stroked Tilly's soft wavy hair and gazed down into her deep blue eyes. 'You make me laugh you do. How could you believe I'd have anything to do with Jamie Thistlewaite? It'll be a good few years before he's released from prison. You must remember Jamie Sonning-Smythe. We bumped into him in Hyde Park a while back. He's one of my old university friends. His father's loaded, and they come from this neck of the woods. I just put two and two together and asked for some help. I needed someone to confide in when you upped and left for New York. Jamie was able to fill in some of the gaps about Pebblestown, like your grandfather naming it in the first place.'

Theo unclasped his briefcase and handed the newspaper cutting to Matilda who read it in a state of shock. 'I can't believe you've gone to all this trouble to meet my family.'

Theo looked out of the window at Arthur and Fluffy making their way back to the pebblestone cottage. 'It was just a whim at first. I felt near to you by being here but things have escalated, and I've been drawn into more obscure scenarios than I could ever have imagined. Being here is making life in London seem dull. Your grandfather even asked me to woo Lady Leticia at one point.'

Matilda burst into tears of laughter; washing all the sadness and frustration of the last few months away. 'That's Grandpa for you. There must have been a good reason for that one. What was he trying to achieve that time?'

It was now Theo's turn to laugh. 'Oh, just to get rid of Edgar Trueman and he well and truly succeeded.'

13

READY FOR GLAMPING

The first weekend in June arrived and with all four Glamping huts fully refurbished it was time to open for business. Three of the huts were booked on a discounted basis by the builders and their families. Arthur thought this was a perfect solution. If there were any problems with the shower and toilet block, then they could be fixed there and then. The fourth hut had been reserved free of charge. It did well to keep on the best side of friends in high places, and Arthur had pulled out all the stops, with Lady Leticia's help, to bring a luxurious touch to the Summer hut which would be used for the weekend by Jamie.

With building work still ongoing at the public house, delicatessen and bistro, facilities in Truelove

Hills were considerably lacking, and Jamie wandered into Cindy's Bakery to buy something for dinner. Cindy's bright blue eyes widened at the sight of the tall, tanned stranger and her long blonde ponytail swished behind her as she cleared one of the tables on her way back to the counter.

'Hello, my name's Jamie. I'm staying up at Pebble Peak for the weekend in a Glamping hut, and I must admit that I've not come prepared. There are several families up there, and they've brought disposable barbecues and cool boxes full of food and I've just turned up. So, I feel a bit out of place. I'm looking forward to trying out the facilities though, it makes a change from living out of hotels and, before you say it, I know the chateau has a restaurant, but I somehow feel that would be "cheating" to go there for dinner.'

Cindy smiled at this man who oozed charm, confidence and good manners. 'Hello Jamie, it's good to meet you. I'm Cindy Copperfield, and this is my bakery. Well, it's my bakery for just another three weeks. I'm moving into new premises at the end of the month. Maybe next time you visit our Glamping facility, you can come to dine in my new bistro. That won't be as posh as the chateau and certainly wouldn't be considered "cheating" if you wanted to go out for a meal during your stay in Truelove Hills.'

Jamie held back his dark blonde hair in both hands, and his turquoise eyes scanned the limited supplies left in the bakery at nearly five o'clock in the afternoon. Cindy had an idea. 'I could make a picnic if you like and bring it up to Pebble Peak this evening. How many of you are staying in your hut?'

Jamie turned around to face her with a better idea. 'There's just me, but if you're available this evening, then we could have a picnic for two. It's ridiculous really, I'm staying in that hut on my own but I've somehow been given the celebrity treatment, and there's a fridge stocked with champagne, wine and olives. I thought I'd better come in here to buy a sandwich and a pasty to go with all that alcohol, but if you would care to join me for a picnic this evening there is nothing I'd like more.'

Cindy held onto the counter. 'Well, I am available this evening as it happens.'

Jamie opened his wallet and took out a fifty-pound note. 'I'm afraid I've got nothing smaller in sterling. I've got some euros and dollars, but I'm all out of my very own currency, I've been away a lot.' He looked embarrassed, and Cindy tried to hand the note back.

'You're providing the drink, so I'll provide the food.'

Jamie clasped her note-holding hand between the two of his. 'Absolutely not. I insist. I haven't paid for this weekend anyway; it's a freebie. The least I can do is refund you for the food.'

When Cindy nodded, Jamie released her hand. She wished she hadn't nodded so soon. 'I'll be off up to the hut now, it's the one named "Summer", shall we say seven o'clock?' Cindy nodded again.

Within five minutes the bakery door opened to the sight of an out of breath Mrs Carruthers. 'Oh, Cindy, I was keen to catch you before you closed.'

'Hello Mrs Carruthers, what can I get for you?'

'Oh, nothing really, I just popped in for a chat. Was that a young man I saw leaving here earlier?'

Cindy's cheeks reddened. 'Yes. His name's Jamie, and he's staying in a Glamping hut this weekend. He's very nice.'

Mrs Carruthers' jaw tightened, and she spoke through clenched teeth, she felt very protective of Cindy since her parents moved to Spain. 'Don't go near him, Cindy. I can't say why. He'll only break your heart. I've read about him on the internet.'

Cindy's heart slumped as she locked the bakery. She'd give the fifty-pound note back when she saw him next. He was bound to come back for it tomorrow after her "no show" tonight. She'll say she had other plans, well she did in a way, Matilda was back and was keen for a catch up so she'd meet up with her and drown her sorrows in the Solent Sea fully-licensed Guest House.

*

At eight o'clock the old friends sat together on the patio of the Solent Sea Guest House overlooking the rolling hills that led up to Pebble Peak. David Makepeace appeared from the kitchen with a bottle of prosecco and two glasses.

'Oh, Tilly, it's so good to see you. I can't believe that you and Theo are an item! You'll have to tell me all about it, and New York too. I want to hear all about New York!'

'Well, I'll fill you in on Theo first. It wasn't love at first sight, in fact, I was so annoyed with him that I chased him down Kensington High Street waving a soggy book!'

Cindy laughed. 'What on earth happened?'

'I was sitting outside a coffee shop writing one of my stories when he stormed past, knocked my drink over and didn't even stop to apologise. Anyway, when I caught up with him, I let him know what I thought of him in no uncertain terms and it was *him* chasing *me* after that. We were together for six months before I went to New York. Never in a million years did I expect to meet up with him again right here in Truelove Hills.'

Cindy's eyes glistened. 'You're so lucky, Tilly. You and Theo are meant to be together; it's obvious – a case of true love if ever I saw one.'

Two hours later the conversation changed to Cindy's news. 'Well, there's so much excitement going on with my business. Theo's had some great ideas and the new bakery, delicatessen and bistro will be ready in three weeks. On the boyfriend front, there's absolutely nothing to say, except that I nearly had a date tonight for the first time in three years.'

Matilda sat forward in her chair. 'You did? What happened?'

Cindy sipped her drink. 'Well, this tanned guy turned up in the shop this afternoon just before closing. He tried to con me into joining him for a picnic up at Pebble Peak in one of the Glamping huts. I had a lucky escape though. Mrs Carruthers warned me off him, she's read all about him on the internet and says I should avoid him at all costs.'

Matilda frowned. 'Is he a builder? Theo will want to know if he is. The builders and their families are staying in three of the huts. Jamie's in the other one.'

Cindy jumped up and knocked her glass over. 'You know him? You know Jamie? What's wrong with him, what's he done?'

'He went to university with Theo. They're great

friends. It's Jamie's father who's investing in the development of Truelove Hills. I wonder what Mrs Carruthers has seen on the internet about him?' Matilda brought the internet up on her phone and typed in his name. Both girls held their breath. Several searches later there was nothing on the internet that was untoward about Jamie.

Cindy slumped back in her chair. 'What am I going to do now? I've stood him up.'

'You're going to take less notice of Mrs Carruthers in future, that's what you're going to do. She obviously overheard me talking to Theo about a different Jamie and got her wires crossed. Don't worry, Theo will smooth things over.'

*

Jamie was snoring, too much wine on an empty stomach meant that his mood in the morning would be far from cordial. He never got stood up. Cindy had undoubtedly grabbed his attention but not in a good way.

14

A FRESH START

It was Saturday morning and busy in the bakery. People from the surrounding towns and villages had come to Truelove Hills for a look around in advance of its full facelift. Cindy's heart missed a beat each time the door opened, but there was no sign of Jamie.

At the Glamping site, the barbecues were fired up again, and the smell of sausages and bacon drifted in through the open windows of the Summer hut, but there was still no sign of Jamie.

At the chateau, a table for two had been laid for breakfast on the terrace overlooking the vast manicured lawns adorned with Italian style sculptures. The butler summoned the guests to their table where their food awaited. Theo stared at Jamie. 'You don't look too good mate. Do you think you could keep some pancakes down? Let me move that fry-up onto the next table.'

Jamie didn't feel like speaking, apart from the fact that his ego was bruised he was nauseous and angry.

'Look, Jamie, it was just a misunderstanding. Tilly says that something came up and Cindy didn't have your mobile number to let you know. She can make the picnic tonight instead. I can get a message to her.'

Jamie's face turned green, and he excused himself from the table. There was no way he wanted to see Cindy today, tonight or even tomorrow. He felt ill and just wanted to go home.

Returning to the table, Jamie ordered toast. Could it be that he hadn't just been stood up for no reason? Maybe Cindy did have a genuine excuse?

One hour later and Jamie was beginning to feel human again. Theo knew his friend's rapid hangover recovery rate from university days; he would be normal by lunchtime. 'Why don't we go for a drive this afternoon, the four of us? Tilly's been dying to spend time with Cindy. One of Tilly's sisters can cover for Cindy at the bakery. Shall I phone the girls now and get things sorted?'

The sparkle was back in Jamie's eyes, and he nodded his approval at Theo. His friend always knew how to win him around. This excuse of Cindy's had better be good.

*

Jamie's vintage convertible Alfa Romeo oozed quality and class. The sun bounced off its silver bonnet and the cream leather seats, which were heated on cold days, didn't need to be activated today – the temperature was hot for June. The girls sat in the back and Theo amused himself with the sound system from the passenger seat next to Jamie. Although the heat poured down from the clear blue sky on the four of them, the atmosphere was cool.

Cindy and Matilda had murmured the briefest of "hello's" before climbing into the back seats and Jamie had just nodded in return. Theo was too interested in the car to notice. 'Let's start it up then! I can't believe your father lends you one of his cars whenever you go to visit. I take it you'll be returning it to Sonning Hall tomorrow before heading back to London.'

Jamie stared in the rear-view mirror at a miserable-looking Cindy. She hadn't even had the decency to explain why she stood him up. She'd just jumped in the car without looking him in the eye. The last thing he wanted today was to have to make conversation with her especially when his father was hosting a Christmas Fair back at the Hall. Jamie looked at the clock on the dashboard it was one-thirty, he could be home in an hour if he called Tristan to arrange it.

Jamie turned in his seat and glanced at the girls. 'I'm afraid I'm double-booked today. The matter simply crossed my mind. My Papa needs me back home for a Christmas Fair, so I'm cutting my visit to Truelove Hills short. Apologies, but I must make a call now to commence the arrangements.'

Cindy's blue eyes narrowed and her face contorted with fury. 'Mrs Carruthers was right about you! How dare you swan into Truelove Hills, charm the pants off of everyone and then just dump us out of your car, your life, as soon as the idea "crosses your mind"! You're not a gentleman; you're a cad and a buffoon who has to borrow his Daddy's cars!!'

The colour drained from Jamie's face. 'What has Mrs Carruthers said about me?'

Matilda held onto Cindy's knotted hands and leant forward to speak to Jamie. 'We're very sorry, Jamie, but Mrs Carruthers got hold of the wrong end of the stick and thought you were supposed to be in prison. She got your name wrong that's all. It's not her fault.'

Jamie raised his eyebrows at Theo who burst out laughing. 'She thought you were Jamie Thistlewaite.'

It was now Jamie's turn to laugh, he threw his head back, and his shoulders shook as relief turned to hilarity. 'I have never heard anything so funny in my life! No wonder you stood me up, Cindy. I forgive you if you forgive me for being a "cad" and a "buffoon".' He looked over his shoulder.

Cindy's face had returned to prettiness, and she raised a blonde eyebrow as she spoke. 'I forgive you, but next time, if there ever is a next time, you need to make up an excuse that's better than a Christmas Fair at Sonning Hall in June.'

Jamie opened his car door and ushered Matilda and Cindy out of the back. 'Go and pack your overnight bags, you need to be back here in fifteen minutes max. My Papa throws the best Christmas parties and the one tonight is not to be missed.'

*

Tristan was waiting at the heliport. He was never far away from Jamie. Lord Sonning-Smythe made sure of that. He paid Tristan a fortune: Bodyguard, pilot, assistant – Tristan was multi-talented and well worth every penny in the Lord's quest to protect his son and heir.

The helicopter touched down, and the foursome removed their seatbelts. Cindy released Jamie's hand which she'd clasped for the whole of the flight. Once she'd reached over to grab it in a moment of panic as the helicopter rose from the ground, she felt too awkward to move it. She could see Jamie's constant grin out of the corner of her eyes and, as he didn't take his hand back for the whole of the short flight, Cindy sensed that their earlier squabbles had been forgotten.

Lord Sonning-Smythe waved from the centre of a tinsel covered balcony on the third floor of Sonning Hall; large Christmas trees adorned each end and alternate angels and stars hung from the balustrade. 'Hello Jamie and friends! Welcome to Sonning Hall! I'll be down with you in two shakes of a reindeer's tail.'

Cindy glanced at Jamie, who this time took hold of *her* hand. 'Don't worry, Papa's quite sane; he just takes the word "eccentric" to a whole new level.'

Theo bowed slightly. He didn't know whether to hold out his hand or not so decided to go with the safer option of lowering his head. Lord Sonning-Smythe slapped him on the back. 'No need for that old chap, a good strong handshake will do and before you ask, call me Clive. My father was a bit of an oddball. Why on earth anyone would want to name a child Cliveden is beyond me.'

Matilda warmed to this giant of a man. He was an older version of Jamie in looks, tall, tanned, turquoise eyes but with silver tones overtaking the remaining dark blonde hair of his youth. 'Hi Clive, I'm Matilda, but you can call me "Tilly". I'll answer to either, but my family and friends shorten it sometimes when I'm in their good books and I quite like it.'

Clive kissed Tilly on both cheeks. 'Now, Tilly, what does this handsome young man over here call you?' Clive nodded towards Theo.

'Oh, Theo calls me Tilly all of the time.'

Clive held out his hand to Theo. 'Good choice old chap. Now, Jamie, are you going to introduce me to *your* young lady?'

Jamie squeezed Cindy's hand before answering. 'Well, Papa, we only met yesterday, but this is Cindy Copperfield. Cindy owns the bakery in Truelove Hills, but as of next month, she's expanding to new premises in the lane opposite the Solent Sea Guest House. You remember the derelict shops I told you about? Well, they're almost renovated, and Cindy's business will be a godsend in catering for the influx of visitors to the village. There's a shortage of eating places to cater for all demands, trust me.'

Clive kissed Cindy on both cheeks too. 'I've heard all about you, Cindy, a real stalwart if ever there was one. Couldn't move on like your friends to pastures new because of your brothers. Your time has come now my girl; your time has come.'

Jamie rubbed his forehead. Theo had briefed him on Truelove Hills and the members of the community, he had been aware of Cindy's loyalty to her family, but he couldn't remember telling his father. He thought he'd only given him a high-level overview of what was required in order to gain his investment. Maybe he had rambled on a bit and gone into more detail; he just couldn't remember.

At that point, it started snowing. Clive clapped his hands in delight. 'Those snow machines never let us down. Now hurry along into the Hall, afternoon tea's waiting; mince pies, yule log, sausage rolls, mulled wine, sherry and snowballs. You have to have a good sausage roll or two at Christmas! The show starts at seven and the party gets going after dark. See you all later.'

15

CHRISTMAS AT SONNING HALL

You better watch out, you better not cry, better not pout, I'm telling you why, cause Santa Claus is coming to town ... There were shrieks of delight from the audience as the music blared out.

Jamie and his friends sat in the front row of the grandstand on one of the back lawns of Sonning Hall. Children surrounded them. Jamie whispered to Cindy: 'This is the children's part of the evening, it's just for the first hour. For the children who have parents or guardians, they may stay on a bit to have a look around the festive stalls, for those that came on one of the coaches they'll leave just after eight as they have further to travel back.'

Cindy's eyes widened. 'Do you mean that some of the children have come here from children's homes?'

'Yes. Papa says that "Christmas is for children".

Since I grew up, he seems to have lost his way at Christmas.'

'You haven't mentioned your mother. Do you have any brothers or sisters?'

'My mother isn't worth a mention. Soon after I was born Papa discovered she was having an affair. She had been all along – with the notorious Edgar Trueman. They'd connived together to fleece Papa of all his money. When Papa found out that was the end of her *and* the reason why I have no siblings. He's never remarried he says he can't trust anyone.'

Cindy turned pale.

'Are you OK Cindy? Do you need a drink?'

Cindy shook her head. 'I'm just shocked, Jamie. Your poor father – poor you.'

'It's not been too bad; Papa and I are very close and at least I don't have any brothers or sisters to fight with when I want to borrow the cars or use the helicopter. There are some definite advantages to being an only child.' Jamie winked, and Cindy smiled up at him. She pinched herself just to check that she wasn't dreaming.

At eight o'clock precisely, Father Christmas appeared on the roof of Sonning Hall. He waved to the children, held his sack in the air, then climbed up a small ladder before disappearing down one of the chimneys. Cindy and Tilly jumped up and joined in with all the children screaming their delight.

Jamie looked up at Cindy; she radiated with sheer joy. He then glanced over at Theo; he was kissing Tilly, and for just a moment in time everything that had ever mattered in the world before now was irrelevant. Maybe there was such a thing as Christmas spirit, Jamie had never experienced it before.

A piercing whistle directed all gazes to the front doors of the Hall. When all the children were quiet, Clive and several of his staff emerged with sacks of presents to go back with the children on the coaches and balloons for those that were staying for the further festivities. Tilly would know that whistle anywhere. She jumped down from the grandstand and marched past Clive and his staff into the foyer of Sonning Hall. 'Grandpa, what on earth are you doing here?'

Arthur twisted his silver moustache and pulled back his red hood with white fur trim before shuffling his shiny black boots. 'Well, now Matilda, how was I supposed to know you were going to be here?'

Theo, Cindy and Jamie arrived seconds later, followed by Clive.

Clive took the lead. 'Arthur's an old friend of mine. I run several events during the year for people, well, people who are a bit lonely. Arthur popped along a few years back, and we've been as thick as thieves ever since. If there's one person I trust in this world, it's him. Arthur's filled me in on the latest antics of that rogue Edgar Trueman, and between the pair of us we came up with a cunning plan to stop him taking over Pebblestown. We couldn't get away with the name change in the end, but we both see the potential in it.'

Matilda stood with hands on hips. 'So, tell us your cunning plan.'

Arthur looked at the sky. 'I asked my Alice for inspiration. She said that Lady Leticia wouldn't want her castle turned into a casino, so Clive and I decided to go with that.'

It was now Theo's turn to raise his eyebrows. 'So, are you telling us that Edgar Trueman had no plans to turn the chateau into a casino?'

Arthur and Clive nodded in unison.

Jamie slowly clapped his hands. 'I have to give it to you. You two are a force to be reckoned with.'

Tristan arrived with a bottle of champagne and a tray of glasses. 'With the compliments of your staff, Lord Clive. We wanted to thank you for the very sumptuous Christmas lunch you kindly provided for everyone today. The caterers have just left in advance of the coaches making their way down the lanes to the motorway.'

Matilda grabbed Cindy's arm before whispering. 'Clive paid for caterers to feed his staff?!' She then turned her attention to her grandfather. Taking him to one side, she looked him straight in the eyes. 'You're very naughty, Grandpa. You've hidden behind Grandma to get your way. You shouldn't have blamed the casino idea on her.'

Arthur knew how to handle Matilda. 'Well, who'd have gone with it if it was my idea? Pretty good one though wasn't it? It did the job. Your grandmother will be looking down on us laughing. I need a bit of inspiration from her now, or from anyone close to her, about what to do with all those pebble hearts I've made. I've trained Fluffy to take them to the Lady's castle up the hill. My first thought was to provide a bit of romance up there to live up to the "Truelove Hills" image. We've only had the opportunity to do it once though as Leticia's only had a couple of guests.'

'Oh, Grandpa! You didn't start a rumour between my boss and his assistant, did you?!'

Arthur winked.

It was a minute before Matilda hugged him. 'Well, I must say your ideas are second to none. Grandma would be proud of you, and I love you so very much.'

*

Following a spectacular firework display, the Christmas

Fair at Sonning Hall came to a close. A Rolls Royce made its way to the front of the building, and Clive turned to Arthur. 'Father Christmas, your car awaits.'

Arthur shook Clive's hand. 'Look after those youngsters for me. I want at least three of them back by tomorrow afternoon. Your son's always welcome to visit us of course.'

The chauffeur opened the door, and Arthur climbed inside. 'Make sure you drop me off in the usual place. I don't want any prying eyes in the village.'

The journey was over two hours by car. Arthur settled back into the comfortable upholstery, and by the time they were at the end of Sonning Hall's drive, he was asleep.

16

FINAL PREPARATIONS

With the Glamping site up and running, it was now the turn of the public house re-opening and the relocation of Cindy's Bakery to her new extended premises. The last week of June had arrived, and chaos reigned.

Cindy felt the need to scream at her brothers but managed to keep her composure. 'Steve, you need to stop helping out at the pub and put those shelves up in the delicatessen. Bruce, you need to get up off the sofa and get your backside into gear. Is there nothing that gets you going? I am certainly not going to work around the clock to keep you two in designer trainers for the rest of your lives that's for sure.'

The sirens could be heard from a distance at first; then they became louder until the blue lights of an ambulance brought the residents of Truelove Hills out of their homes.

'Make way, make way!' A stretcher was carried into the public house.

Thirty minutes passed before the paramedics emerged with an empty stretcher and drove off in the ambulance.

Mrs Carruthers was aghast. She held herself up by clinging onto Cindy's arm. 'It's not good news. A funeral car will arrive in a minute, one of those blacked-out things to remove bodies. Someone's died, and they won't be bothered taking a corpse in an ambulance. I know these things, trust me.'

With Cindy's Bakery closed for removals, the best place for everyone to congregate was in the Solent Sea Guest House. Mrs Carruthers needed a brandy, so she poured one from behind the bar in the guest lounge.

Cindy surveyed the room, none of the Makepeace's were there, and neither was Theo. She had tried to call Matilda, but there was no answer. Her heart sank. Bruce leant over the bar and poured himself a brandy too. Cindy scowled at him. It must be Arthur; Fluffy was nowhere in sight. What a tragedy just a few days before all the visitors were due to arrive.

The door to the guest house flew open, and Steve wandered in, a look of surprise on his face. Cindy lurched forwards. 'Steve, were you in the pub when it happened?'

He blinked at the mass of eyes glaring at him. 'I sure was.' Everyone slumped in their chairs or back against the walls from standing positions.

Bruce poured two more brandies; one for him, one for Steve. Bruce knocked his back, and Steve sipped his.

With a shaking hand, Mrs Carruthers held out her glass for a top up. 'Have they said when the funeral will be?'

Steve blinked again like a rabbit in the headlights. He took his time to process what was going on before speaking. 'She doesn't need a funeral yet, she only fainted.'

Bruce slammed his glass on the bar. 'Who? Who fainted?'

Steve shrugged his shoulders. 'Your girlfriend; Tallulah Makepeace.'

Bruce ran from the room, and Mrs Carruthers felt a warm glow in her stomach. She'd seen that boy entering the guest house by the back door on many a night. Mrs Carruthers didn't know which twin he'd been after though and with all the excitement about that rogue Jamie Thistlewaite, there was far too much gossip for her to keep on top of. That reminded her, there was a letter from HM Prison addressed to Lady Leticia at the chateau that she'd steamed open earlier today. It was from that evil Edgar Truman. He was "inside" now and asking for forgiveness. The Lady didn't need to know about that, things were going far too well in Truelove Hills, and now that Arthur wasn't dead, things were really looking up!

There was so much to do, and so little time. Cindy was reeling from the news of Bruce and Tallulah. Why hadn't she realised? Still, it was *her* time now. Clive had said *her* time had come. She grabbed her remaining brother by his arm. 'Come on; I need your help. Once you've put up the shelves, we need to empty all the boxes – we only have four days before we open.'

Steve patted his sister's hand. 'I'm always here for you Sis, I always have been. We can do this together without that lump of lard getting in the way.'

*

Bruce stared at Tallulah lying on one of the newly upholstered benches in the public house. She opened her eyes and glared at him. 'I'm pregnant OK. I'm flaming pregnant!' She closed her eyes and tears streamed down her translucent cheeks, she turned over on her side her flame red hair covering her face, the curls nearly reaching the floor.

Bruce looked back just once before he left the pub and Truelove Hills forever.

17

TIME TO REFLECT

David Makepeace took full responsibility for Tallulah's "funny turn". He'd been working the twins too hard in the run-up to the pub's re-opening. Those Copperfield boys had been helpful, but now the older one had disappeared off the face of the earth. You couldn't get the staff these days. Still, the pub was nearly ready, so David arranged for Tabitha and Tallulah to have a night away in London.

David drove his daughters to the station. 'Enjoy your last chance of freedom for a while. Once the pub's opened, you'll be rushed off your feet.'

Tabitha climbed out of the car and hugged her father. 'This is so kind of you, Daddy. We'll be back all refreshed for Opening Day.'

Tallulah pulled her overnight bag off the back seat. 'There's really no need for this. I'm not drinking anyway, so no late night for me, I feel washed out.'

Tabitha waited until they were seated on the train to tackle her miserable sister. 'What's wrong with you, Tallulah? You worry us all by fainting, and now you're being so ungrateful to Daddy, who's never given us a treat like this before. It must be costing a fortune to put us up in a Spa Hotel in London. If you're sulking because Bruce Copperfield has deserted us at the worst time he could choose to; then you're stupid. He's no good that one. I'm pleased he's gone away. I was worried you two might start having a fling.'

Tallulah shrugged her shoulders and Tabitha decided not to push the subject. 'I'll just go out on my own tonight then. You can go to bed.'

*

Cindy questioned Steve: 'So how long's Bruce been seeing Tallulah? Why's he run away? Why didn't you tell me what was going on?'

Steve turned down the TV sound on the remote. Cindy was like a Rottweiler when she wanted information on her brothers. This wasn't going to be an easy conversation. 'I didn't tell you anything because I didn't know myself. I only suspected he fancied her and by calling her his "girlfriend" in front of that room full of people and the reaction that got from him, I must be right. She's probably dumped him, and his pride's taken a knock. He'll turn up once he's got over it.'

*

By the time the twins checked into their hotel, there was a change in Tallulah. 'Don't you even think about going out tonight without me. I'm feeling much better now. You're right; it would be a shame to waste a treat like this.'

Tallulah unpacked her bag and Tabitha pulled open the door to the minibar in their room. 'There's chocolate in here as well as alcohol. What can I interest you in?'

'Oh, chocolate definitely and a soft drink. I'll have some wine later. I'm still a bit scared after passing out in the pub. I can't believe that Daddy called for an ambulance. I just needed sitting up with my head between my knees. Still, we wouldn't be here now if I hadn't caused such a scene.'

Tabitha smiled; she'd got her sister back. It was always best to leave her alone for a while when she was in one of her sulks.

*

After dinner, the twins decided to give a trip to a

nightclub a miss. Tabitha sighed. 'Can you believe we're only 21? When we were at art school, we didn't get back to our apartment until at least two in the morning during the week. Do you think we've worn ourselves out too soon?'

Tallulah yawned. 'Well, if we're old before our time then there's no hope for Hannah. She must be burnt out by now with her high-powered job, *and* she's nine years older than us.'

Back in their hotel room, Tallulah went to bed, and Tabitha poured a glass of wine from the minibar. She opened the French windows and stepped onto a small balcony overlooking the Thames. London was magical at night. Fairy lights hung between the lamp posts; the London Eye was lit up in shades of red white and blue, and the amber lights of the Palace of Westminster streamed through the windows before reflecting on the rippling surface of the river. The balcony was a good place for people watching and Tabitha sat down on one of the wrought iron chairs to admire the view.

*

Tallulah pulled the bedcovers off her sister. 'What time did you come to bed last night? I went downstairs for breakfast over an hour ago. We'll get you a cake and coffee at the station, that should perk you up. Come on – we need to leave in half an hour.'

One hour later the twins sat in a station café. Tabitha stared out of the window; her head was thumping. 'Don't let me drink ever again.'

Tallulah laughed. 'I've heard that one before. You'll be on the cider once the pub opens.'

'I mean it, Tallulah. I've been hallucinating.'

'Now, you're going to have to explain that one to me. What's happened?'

'I've been dreaming things. I thought I saw Bruce Copperfield standing by the Thames last night and now a woman has just walked past the window that's a striking resemblance to Hannah.'

Tallulah stood up and peered out of the window. 'I can't see anyone that looks like Hannah. We were talking about her yesterday, she's obviously on your mind.'

*

Tabitha slept on the train and was silent in the taxi from the station to Truelove Hills. Tallulah grabbed both their bags and pushed open the door to the pub. 'Hi everyone, we're home!'

David Makepeace and Steve Copperfield were polishing the bar in readiness for Opening Day. Tallulah dropped the bags and Tabitha peered around the door to be met by the widest of smiles from Steve

Copperfield. 'It's good to see you, Tabitha. Are you free tonight to try out some of Cindy's recipes in the bistro? She suggested I ask you.'

Tabitha glanced at Tallulah before responding to Steve. 'Will you be going too?'

'Well, yes, if that's OK. Cindy's keen to do a trial run before the bistro opens.'

Tabitha's mouth fell open, and Tallulah tutted, well that was the end of her sister's abstinence from alcohol; she'd need a drink if she was going out with Steve Copperfield.

A shiver ran down Tallulah's spine, where was Bruce? She wished she hadn't shared her secret; if she hadn't told him, he'd never have gone away.

18

PROPOSALS TO MAKE

With Cindy's Bakery now empty on the High Street, it was time for Theo to put his plans in place to turn the premises into something new. He'd already gained the approval of the parish council. He just needed to seal the deal with the most important person in the world to him. The builders were on standby to work through the next three days and nights to transform the bakery into a gift shop. On the last day of June, the shop was ready.

Theo was both excited and nervous. What if Tilly didn't like the shop? What if she didn't want her own business? What if she wanted to leave Truelove Hills again? What if she didn't want *him*? There was no other way to find out than to go over to the Solent Sea Guest House and blindfold her.

'Theo what are you doing? Why are you tying your scarf around my face? This isn't funny!'

Theo held Tilly by her shoulders. 'Do you trust me?'

'Yes, of course.'

'Do you love me?'

'Unconditionally.'

'Well then, you've nothing to fear. Just take one small step at a time, and I will lead you to our future.' Theo had a last-minute feeling of panic. 'You *do* want to spend the future with me, don't you? We're the next Arthur and Alice, aren't we?'

Tilly smiled beneath the scarf which covered most of her face. 'Well, I'm not sure anyone could compare, but we could give it a damn good go!'

Theo kissed the top of her head. 'I love you Tilly Makepeace, and you're never going to get away from me again ever, no matter how hard you try.'

He was going to do the next bit later, but became lost in the moment and reached into his pocket for a ring. He took hold of Tilly's left hand and "sealed the deal" by placing it on her finger. 'Will you marry me, Tilly?'

Tilly jumped in surprise. 'This is all over the place,

Theo. It isn't exactly how I'd dreamt things would happen. You've covered my face with your scarf and put a ring on my finger before I've even seen it. It could be a ring-pull off one of the fizzy drink cans in the pub for all I know. If this is a test about how much I trust you, then I hope I've passed because the answer is "Yes!".'

Theo whooped loudly and punched the air. He would have preferred to have seen her face at such a special time. He hadn't planned it this way but what's done was done. 'Now follow my lead and tread carefully, our future is just a few steps away.'

Outside the empty shop, Theo removed his scarf and Tilly held up her hand to watch the light bouncing off a large diamond ring. It glinted in the reflection of the glass window before her. She could see that her hair was all over the place yet Theo was looking down at her with admiration.

There was a rope hanging down by the door of the shop, and Theo asked Tilly to pull it. She did so, to reveal the sign: "Matilda's Memorabilia". Her hands flew to her mouth.

Theo tried to explain. 'I want you to be doing what makes you happy. You can write your stories and books in the shop when there are no customers. You could even sell them in here. The village needs a gift shop, and you would be perfect to run it. You were born here and know all the residents and the area. We could live in the apartment upstairs, it would free up a room at the guest house, and Mrs Carruthers is sure to find another tenant easily.'

Tilly didn't comment she just stared into the empty shop. Theo had a contingency plan. 'If you don't like the shop, then we can change the name, and it can be used as something else. There will be plenty of work around in the village once the visitors start coming.'

Tilly pushed open the door and surveyed her surroundings. The shelves were empty, but her heart was full. 'It's just perfect, Theo, just perfect! I love the name "Memorabilia". I promise I will make this work. I'll need Grandpa's help to supply authentic material to sell and, of course, it will have to start with some pebbles. Those hearts he's made will be the first things in my window.'

Theo sighed with relief. 'Your grandfather knew you'd have some brilliant ideas for the shop and your father too.'

Tilly raised her eyebrows. 'They know about the shop?'

'Well, I had to state my intentions when I asked for your hand in marriage. I asked your father first and then your grandfather. I think they were keener for you to run your own business here in Truelove Hills than to end up marrying me; so, I got away easily with their approval.'

Tilly chuckled. 'Don't be silly. You know they love you. We'd better pop over the road and let them know that I've accepted your offer. I'll aim to open the shop in two weeks. That should give Grandpa enough time to make a few more items for my window display. I'll need the twins to help with painting something on the window like: "OPENING SOON – Authentic Artefacts to order; Personalised Souvenirs; Tales of Truelove Hills – original short stories; Local Artwork" – the twins could supply me with paintings to sell for them. This is turning into a real family business!'

*

Mrs Carruthers was struggling to keep her secret. Cindy had been avoiding her since she warned her off Jamie Thistlewaite. If that was the price to pay for keeping the girl safe, then Mrs Carruthers would have to live with it for now. Still, she wouldn't need to keep her secret for much longer, the rogue hadn't been sniffing around the village for over three weeks, and the renovation work was just about complete which meant that the funding must be in place. There was something she could do in the meantime though, just to make sure Jamie didn't turn up here again and that was to get a message from one rogue to another. Mrs Carruthers sent an anonymous letter to HM Prison addressed to Edgar Trueman.

It read:

'Tell Jamie Thistlewaite to stay away from Truelove Hills, or else!'

19

OPEN FOR BUSINESS

The 1st of July had arrived, and the residents of Truelove Hills congregated outside the Village Hall. Lady Leticia Lovett took to the microphone. 'On behalf of the parish council, I would like to thank the residents for their patience, the builders for all their hard work and Lord Sonning-Smythe for his very kind investment in our community. Where is he? Where's the Lord?'

Arthur waved a hand in the air. 'He's running late. His son's on his way back from London. They'll be here for two-thirty in time for the opening of the pub.'

Lady Letitia continued: 'Thank you, Arthur. I must say that I am absolutely thrilled with the redevelopment of Truelove Hills. It has been tasteful, authentic and in keeping with our little part of southern

England; our picturesque hideaway akin to Provence or Tuscany. Truelove Hills is truly unique.'

Two things were bothering Mrs Carruthers, and she needed to tackle them now: 'May I ask where all the visitors are? I thought we were supposed to be open for business from today. I've got a fresh supply of flowers in the General Store, Theo said we needed a florist, so I volunteered to enhance my business accordingly.'

Lady Lovett twisted her pearl earrings and ran a hand over her blonde bun. 'Well, it's early days yet. We have some bookings for later in the month when the school holidays start. The best way to increase business is by word of mouth. So, I suggest we all act with exemplary behaviour, live and breathe the utmost customer service skills and prove to England and the United Kingdom as a whole that we mean business.'

Mrs Carruthers sniffed at that. 'I have another question. I thought our investor was called Jamie Thistlewaite not Lord Sonning something. What happened to Jamie?'

Theo stepped forward. 'I think there has been some confusion over our investor's name. Lord Sonning-Smythe has provided all of the funding to enable us to undertake the renovations in the village. His son, Jamie Sonning-Smythe, has been the hands-on link with the parish council. Jamie has visited

Truelove Hills twice already, and he'll be here again this afternoon with his father.'

Cindy elbowed Mrs Carruthers in the ribs. 'You got the wrong Jamie, Mrs Carruthers. I'm still annoyed with you, so annoyed in fact that I couldn't be bothered putting you right!'

*

At two-thirty a chauffeur-driven black Bentley pulled up outside the public house. The High Street was now pedestrianised, but it had been agreed by the parish council that VIPs and emergency vehicles would be granted access.

Lord Sonning-Smythe emerged from the vehicle to the cheers and whistles of the grateful community. He waved and stopped to survey every single one of the smiling faces. His eyes landed on one face that wasn't smiling at all. The woman was flushed; her eyes didn't meet his, and she had two buckets of flowers at her feet. Jamie suppressed a chuckle. Mrs Carruthers was in a sticky position, he could make things worse for her, but that wasn't in his nature instead he beckoned her over to meet the Lord. 'Papa, this is Mrs Carruthers, she's a pillar of the community. Where would everyone be without a Post Office & General Store and Theo tells me she's now the local florist too.'

Lord Sonning-Smythe shook Mrs Carruthers' hand

with vigour. 'What a woman! An entrepreneur if ever there was one. The village certainly needs your get up and go!'

Cindy sniggered behind her hand to Matilda. 'I sometimes wish she'd just "get up and go".'

Mrs Carruthers looked back at the two buckets. They were standing where she'd left them. She had planned to throw the flowers at the Lady, bunch by bunch, and then empty the mouldy water over that annoying bun of hers. Leticia hadn't been raising awareness of the new Truelove Hills, Mrs Carruthers was sure of it. She'd gone on the internet just yesterday and couldn't find any mention of such a place. The lack of visitors on "Open Day" just confirmed her suspicions.

Anyway, that was for another day. Mrs Carruthers was now in the limelight. Jamie had seen through to the core of her, and she took great satisfaction in that. She was indeed a "Pillar of the Community", that title suited her to a tee.

Lady Leticia emitted a small cough, and the Lord turned to face her. 'You must be Lady Leticia Lovett. I would recognise you anywhere, I've heard so much about you from my good friend Arthur over the years.' The Lady wilted under the gaze of Clive's turquoise eyes and all thoughts of what was supposed to happen next escaped her.

Arthur tutted and stepped to the front of the crowd to take over proceedings. 'As you all know, this village has been without a pub for many years. A pub is the heart of the community. It's a place for people to meet, share stories, play a game of cards or dominoes, it's just somewhere for people to go when they feel happy or sad or . . . lonely. I am delighted to announce this afternoon that my son, David Makepeace, is going to fill that gap. He's been working hard to bring the heart of the village back to life. I'll now pass you over to Clive, who's going to announce the name of the pub.'

Lord Sonning-Smythe wasn't surprised to witness a sea of astounded faces. 'Thank you, Arthur, for calling me by my preferred name, I encourage you all to use it. It would make me feel part of this excellent community. Now, without further ado, I'd like to announce that this Public House – the KING ARTHUR – is officially open for business!' Clive pulled on a cord, and the pub's sign was displayed in all its glory.

There were cheers, and whoops from the residents and Clive placed an arm around Arthur's shoulders. 'I don't know if you can see it without your glasses old mate, but the sign reads: *"KING ARTHUR of Pebblestown".*'

Arthur blinked away a tear. 'I can see it all right, I can see it.'

Matilda and Tabitha rushed over to embrace their grandfather and Tallulah watched from her new bedroom above the pub. She was still shocked by Bruce Copperfield's response to her pregnancy news. What kind of a man was he to just run away? Tallulah blew her nose and vowed to give him no further thought. He'd shown his true colours, it was lucky that during her trip to London she'd discovered it had been a false alarm.

Clive turned on his heels and went on the hunt for Mrs Carruthers who was in the queue to get served at the newly opened bar. David Makepeace and Steve Copperfield were pulling pints a bit too slowly for her liking, besides that Steve should be helping his sister out, not working in the pub. 'Mrs Carruthers! I'd like to do you a deal.' Clive slipped four fifty-pound notes into her hand before whispering. 'I've been admiring those flowers in your buckets, I've no idea what they cost but hopefully this should cover it.'

Mrs Carruthers couldn't believe her luck. First, Jamie had forgiven her and now his father was being so generous. There were some good people about after all. She felt a warmth surround her, it was good being a pillar of the community, all her concerns about never being appointed to the parish council were wiped away. Mrs Carruthers was esteemed in her own right and she would uphold her position with the utmost honesty and integrity.

20

FLOWERS FOR A LADY

After placing the flowers in the boot of the Bentley and giving a nod to Clive, the chauffeur stood by the open back door of the limousine. Clive then made his move. 'My dear Lady Lovett, would you allow me to offer you a ride back to Chateau Amore de Pebblio?'

'Oh, please call me "Leticia" and, yes, I would very much appreciate a lift back to my chateau. There is one condition though – you must stay for afternoon tea.'

*

Afternoon tea passed in a flash and Clive accepted Leticia's offer of dinner. He'd noticed the piano at the bottom of the grand staircase, and he insisted that he paid for her hospitality by "tinkling on the ivories".

Leticia was in raptures, was there nothing this fine specimen of a man could turn his hand to? As she relaxed on a gold satin chaise longue, the butler arranged the buckets of flowers into vases on a table beneath the stairs.

The piano playing at an end, Clive moved to sit next to Leticia, and he held her hand before looking directly into her eyes. 'I admire you, Leticia, you run the chateau as a first-class business, it is second to none in the area, and it needs to be full of people; and by that, I mean paying guests, not just staff. You will never survive once the funds from the sale of your late husband's property portfolio have been extinguished.'

Leticia sat bolt upright, her face crimson and her mouth open to speak. Clive stood up. 'Let me continue. As far as I see it, there's just one thing missing from the success of your business and the future of Truelove Hills, and that's visibility. I know you have taken on the role of raising awareness of the facilities on offer but whatever PR firm you are using should be fired. Your strength lies in hospitality. Truelove Hills needs a Head of Tourism who could be funded out of the profits of each and every business. It's a win-win solution, and it would free you up to focus on this marvellous chateau.'

The weight started shifting from the Lady's shoulders. 'After I lost my husband and then Edgar, I decided to do everything myself. I've obviously not been doing a very good job of it. How did you know about my late husband's property portfolio?'

Clive's eyes twinkled. 'I know Arthur. I also know who would be your perfect Head of Tourism.' Leticia raised her eyebrows, and Clive divulged his thoughts: 'Theo.'

The butler put down his secateurs and tip-toed down the corridor. He needed to make a phone call, and he needed to make it quick.

*

Edgar Trueman was managing to stay quite active in the business world from inside his prison cell. The mobile phone he kept hidden under his toupee was constantly vibrating, and several inmates had the means to relay messages to the outside. Edgar had even bumped into someone in the pottery class this morning who knew Jamie Thistlewaite. It had been a surprise getting a message in the post for him, but at least he'd managed to pass it on even though Jamie had escaped from prison two days before.

There it went again, someone else trying to phone him. Edgar lifted his wig and slid the phone out by his ear. 'Edgar, it's me. There's a Lord Sonning-Smythe who's set on scuppering our plans. You need to get it sorted quick. I'll be in touch with more details.'

The butler ended the call at the sound of footsteps down the hallway.

Mrs Carruthers had only popped into the chateau to retrieve her flower buckets, but she got more than she'd bargained for. The butler was in cahoots with Edgar Trueman and as a pillar of the community she needed to stop it.

*

Back at the King Arthur Mrs Carruthers decided to confide in Theo and Jamie who were propping up the bar. 'There's something funny going on, I've just been up to the chateau, and the butler was on the phone talking to Edgar Trueman. Edgar's inside now along with that Jamie Thistlewaite. I've got a bad feeling about all of this. You two need to do something.'

Jamie grinned at Theo. 'Let us buy you a drink, Mrs Carruthers, then you can tell us all about the old days in Truelove Hills. Cindy says you've been here forever. She can't remember any time when you weren't in the thick of things. You must have some tales to divulge, I'm sure.'

Four double brandies later and Mrs Carruthers had forgotten all about the butler, and Edgar Trueman had never been further from her mind.

*

Jamie Thistlewaite was intrigued. Why was someone telling him to stay away from Truelove Hills? He'd never even heard of the place. In his thirties and bald he was instantly recognisable in the mug shot the police had given to the Press. The plot had started to thicken now though, and some guy called Edgar Trueman was offering advice and help. Firstly, he'd suggested a reputable wig-maker then he'd advised him about a shed in the field at the back of the Solent Sea Guest House in Truelove Hills that was never used. Edgar said that could be a starting point for Jamie until he mailed some cash addressed to him as "Jake Thimbleton" to the Post Office & General Store. All Jamie had to do was to find out what someone called Lord Sonning-Smythe was planning with Lady Lovett, and as a bonus, there was an "insider" at the chateau; the butler. "Jake" couldn't believe his luck.

*

Leticia and Clive sipped champagne over dinner in celebration of their union. Leticia made it quite clear that she wanted nothing more than friendship. Her brief association with Edgar Trueman had put her off men for life. Clive was more than happy with that; he just wanted to help a Lady in distress, and he had too many activities going on with his large circle of friends to have any time for a relationship. After many years as a single man, he was at a point in his life where he was content with how things had turned out.

Leticia held her glass in the air. 'To us, Clive, to us. I have a good feeling that we're onto a winner. With your support, Truelove Hills cannot fail.'

21

AN UNWELCOME VISITOR

It was the 9th of July and Arthur had been working around the clock for over a week to produce authentic artefacts for Matilda's shop. He headed out again just after eight in the morning to start work in his shed. He pushed the door open and sat down at his workbench.

Jake stood behind a storage cupboard holding a large chisel. Arthur bent over the pebblestone fruit bowl he'd been making since yesterday and whistled while he worked. Jake twisted in his confined space and dropped the chisel. Arthur rose to full height and picked up the largest mallet on the table. 'Who's there? Come out now, or fear for your life!'

Jake edged out into the open and Arthur put down his mallet. He surveyed the man. His hands and face were streaked with grime, his shaggy brown hair hadn't seen shampoo for some time, and his grey eyes were cold and lost.

Arthur sighed. 'It's not all of us who've been so fortunate in life. Let me help you. If you come with me up to Pebble Peak, you can use the shower and toilet facilities and stay in one of the Glamping huts for a couple of days. Theo will lend you some clothes and Leticia will see you're all right for food.'

Jake stood rooted to the spot. 'Theo?'

'Yes, Theo Tressler, he's a good boy. Used to work in London as a stockbroker. His heart brought him here. He's engaged to my granddaughter, Matilda. He's just landed himself a key role in Truelove Hills as Head of Tourism. Leticia and Clive decided upon that. That's, Lady Lovett and Lord Sonning-Smythe to you. Things have come a long way since we got rid of Edgar Trueman. You won't have heard of him but, let me tell you, he's always up to no good so if you ever bump into him on your travels quickly scarper in the other direction at all costs. That's my advice.'

Jake wiped his hand on his trouser leg before holding it out. 'I don't know your name.'

'Apologies for that, I'm Arthur Makepeace. What's your name?'

'Jamie. I need to collect a letter from the Post Office, can you show me where it is?'

'Of course, we'll pop in on our way up to Pebble

Peak. I'll introduce you to Mrs Carruthers.'

Mrs Carruthers didn't like the look of the scruffy man standing before her, and his voice belied his outer appearance. 'I'm pleased to meet you, Mrs Carruthers. Do you have a letter for me my name's Jake Thimbleton?'

'How do I know you are who you say you are?'

Jake lifted his torn shirt sleeve to display the initials "JT" tattooed on the top of his left arm in the middle of a design that depicted a group of tall buildings.

'Have you got a passport, driving licence, any other form of identity?'

Arthur twisted his moustache. He'd promised to pick up Fluffy from Tallulah at nine o'clock. Tallulah had taken to going for long morning walks, and Fluffy was up for every minute of it. 'Look at the poor man. He's in no fit state to lie about his name. Just give him the envelope, and I'll get him washed, brushed up and then locked up in one of the Glamping huts.' Arthur glanced sideways at Jake. 'You'll have your own key of course.'

Fluffy and Tallulah were coming down the hill as Arthur and Jake walked up. 'Thanks, Tallulah, Fluffy can have an extra bit of exercise this morning by coming with us now up to Pebble Peak. He winked at his granddaughter and Fluffy jumped up at Jake to take a good sniff of his trousers. 'Now get yourself straight home, your father will need you at the King Arthur no doubt.'

Tallulah stopped by the Post Office & General Store first. 'What do you think of that man that's with Grandpa, Mrs Carruthers?'

Mrs Carruthers was already on the internet. 'I don't like him at all, Tallulah. I think he's into money laundering. There was two thousand pounds in that envelope addressed to him; I steamed it open yesterday. Not only that, I recognised his eyes, it's a long shot now but . . . here we go! No wonder he's got a tattoo on his arm with the initials "JT" by a drawing of Canary Wharf – his name's not Jake Thimbleton it's Jamie Thistlewaite, and he's on the run from prison!'

Tallulah screamed and rushed out into the High Street. Mrs Carruthers ran after her. 'Let's get you home and then I need to get some help for your grandfather.'

There was a Ferrari parked in the car park of the Glamping site, bright red and gleaming with power – and the keys were in the ignition. Jake knocked Arthur to the ground and jumped into the car. Fluffy jumped in after him. A man was asleep in the passenger seat. These were distractions Jake didn't need. He'd dump the man and the dog once he'd got far enough away. There was no need to keep the deal with Edgar Trueman now; he'd got enough money to start him on his new life. The man woke up, and Jake knocked him out with a single punch. Fluffy bared his teeth and bit into Jake's arm, the Ferrari spun, and Jake stopped the car. He needed to get rid of the dog. He opened his door, grabbed hold of Fluffy and threw him onto the grass verge. The Ferrari roared out of sight.

Mrs Carruthers led the meeting in Matilda's shop. She'd asked Tabitha to keep an eye on Tallulah and the pub and then gone into the Solent Sea Guest House to request David Makepeace's immediate attendance over the road. Matilda and Theo were in Matilda's Memorabilia making final preparations for the shop opening in four days' time.

'You need to be aware that we have an escaped prisoner in our vicinity. He's gone up to Pebble Peak with Arthur. Arthur's just trying to be kind to him because he looks like he's fallen on hard times, but I've worked out who the man really is – he's Jamie Thistlewaite.'

Theo and Matilda sighed; Mrs Carruthers was going out of her mind. Matilda spoke first. 'Not this whole Jamie Thistlewaite thing again, Mrs Carruthers, it's getting tedious now.'

Theo shrugged his shoulders. 'Well, it looks like "Jamie Thistlewaite" is going to finally meet Jamie Sonning-Smythe. Jamie stayed late last night, and we sent him up to the Glamping site rather than drive back to Sonning Hall.'

Mrs Carruthers banged her fist on a shelf then held

her stinging hand, her voice was broken, and tears welled in her eyes. 'You have to believe me. Please believe me. Arthur's in danger, and we need to go up to Pebble Peak.'

22

THE HOSTAGE

Fluffy had made his way back to his master and was howling. They were soon joined by David Makepeace, Matilda, Theo and Mrs Carruthers. Fluffy licked his master's face, and Arthur opened his eyes. Matilda ran into the Summer hut to fetch a pillow. Arthur shook his head; he was seeing a few stars. 'There's no need for that, Tilly, I'm fine. You need to notify the authorities that there's someone about who's no good. He says his name's Jake Thimbleton, but he told me earlier he was called "Jamie".'

Mrs Carruthers raised her nose in the air. 'See, that backs up what I've been saying.'

Theo glanced over to the car park. 'The Ferrari's gone. Jamie must have left early this morning.'

Arthur held his head in both hands. 'No! The rogue

was eyeing up the Ferrari before he knocked me out. He must have driven off in it.'

Theo phoned the police.

*

The Ferrari's fuel light came on, and Jake stopped at a petrol station. He went into the building to pay by cash. The cashier recognised the car, but Jamie Sonning-Smythe had let himself go a bit. 'It's a pleasure to serve you as always Mr Sonning-Smythe. Please give our regards to the Lord when you get back to Sonning Hall.'

Jake nodded. He climbed back into the car and noticed a folder slotted down next to the driver's seat. He pulled it out and looked inside. There were letters and documents; all addressed to Jamie Sonning-Smythe. Jake studied the unconscious man in the passenger seat and released a slow whistle. He'd hit the jackpot this time. He'd unknowingly got himself a hostage of the highest order; the Lord would surely pay a few million pounds for the return of his son.

*

The announcement came on the local radio:

The son and heir of Lord Sonning-Smythe has been kidnapped. Jamie Sonning-Smythe is being held hostage by Jamie Thistlewaite an escaped prisoner convicted of corporate fraud. Lord Sonning-Smythe has agreed to pay the ransom of five million pounds. A time has been set for the release of the hostage at four o'clock this afternoon at a location yet to be decided.

*

Jake turned down the volume of the radio in the Ferrari; his hostage was stirring. The priority was to park the car up somewhere near a derelict building so that they could both go into hiding until the police liaison officer arrived with the ransom at four o'clock.

*

Fluffy was on a mission. He'd got the scent of both men in the Ferrari. No-one was going to harm his master and get away with it. Now that Arthur was back to normal, Fluffy made his way to the chateau and barked at the arched wooden doors.

A maid opened the door for Fluffy. She had become quite fond of him and, as the butler could be slow off the mark to answer the dog's barks, she regularly took the time to let him in and give him a cuddle. 'What do you want today, Fluffy? I'll put you down, and you can show me the way.'

Fluffy sniffed his way to the butler's bedroom. The maid shook her head. 'You can't go in there, Fluffy.' Fluffy pleaded with her with his big black eyes. 'What's bothering you? The butler's not in there he'll be in the dining room at this time of day. Fluffy barked, then whimpered and sat up begging. The maid smiled. 'You're such a funny dog. I'll open the door just a little bit so you can see he's not inside and then we'll need to get you back outside before I get in trouble with the Lady.'

Fluffy pushed through the open door and sniffed his way around the bed. There was a jacket on the floor with a mobile phone half-way out of a pocket. Fluffy bared his teeth and bit into the leather case, he dragged the phone onto the floor and then tipped it up onto its edge so that he could get a good grasp of it in his mouth. With the phone firmly in place, Fluffy ran out of the room in search of the Lady.

Lady Leticia was tending to the flowers on the terrace. She was pleased to be wearing gardening gloves when she extracted the soggy leather case from Fluffy's mouth. 'What have you got for me here, Fluffy? Whose phone is this?' The lady opened the case to the sight of seventeen missed calls, all from Edgar Trueman. She took off her gardening gloves, sat down at the nearest table and reached for a pitcher of water. It was the butler's phone. He hadn't turned up for work this morning, that alone was shocking, but it was absolutely disgraceful that he was in contact with Edgar Trueman behind the Lady's back.

*

The butler regained consciousness in the Ferrari. 'Where am I? Who are you? I only wanted to have a sit in one of these, and the seat was so comfortable I must have fallen asleep.'

Jake swerved the Ferrari to a halt. 'You're Jamie Sonning-Smythe, and you're the heir to a fortune. I'm going to make millions from your father.'

The butler scratched his head. 'My father's been dead for years. Now take me back to the chateau, I'll lose my job if I'm late for my shift.'

Jake heard the helicopters overhead. The police were closing in on him, and he didn't even have the right hostage. He opened the car door and bolted.

*

Jamie phoned Cindy. 'Of course, I'm all right. I had a text message when I got to the Glamping hut last night asking me to attend a meeting in London at eight this morning. I called Tristan to come and get me. I couldn't drive to the heliport as we'd all had a few drinks over dinner. Unfortunately, I left the keys in Papa's Ferrari. I must say the police have been brilliant with all of this, making us all keep quiet about Jamie Thistlewaite having the wrong hostage. I can't believe it turned out to be Leticia's butler!'

*

Lady Leticia handed the butler's phone to the police officers who arrived at the chateau. 'My butler is missing, and I have evidence on his phone that he's in collusion with Edgar Trueman, who's a rotten apple if ever there was one.'

One of the police officers excused himself to take a call on his radio. He returned with news for the Lady. 'We've found your butler, and we've taken him in for questioning. He's been involved in a case of mistaken identity. Unfortunately, an escaped prisoner is still at large.'

Jake wasn't stupid. The last place the police would look for him now was in Truelove Hills. He just needed somewhere to hide until the heat was off.

23

AN UNLIKELY HERO

One week after the unwelcome visit of an escaped prisoner to Truelove Hills, the villagers had returned to normal life. Lady Lovett had advertised for a new butler; Matilda's Memorabilia was attracting customers to the area and, in the process, day visitors were dining at Cindy's Bistro or the King Arthur.

Clive was becoming a regular visitor to the village, apart from taking it upon himself to ensure that Leticia didn't get ripped off again; he enjoyed spending time with Arthur over a pint or two in the pub.

Cindy was rushed off her feet, she'd taken on staff to help with the bakery, delicatessen and bistro and she'd released her brother, Steve, to move to his more natural role of working in the pub with Tabitha and Tallulah. She hadn't heard from Bruce since he disappeared last month, that was a disappointment. Cindy sighed, she wasn't surprised; Steve had always been the most reliable one out of the two.

Mrs Carruthers kept a keen ear to the ground and an eye on the internet. There was nothing that got past her; if any more dodgy characters turned up in Truelove Hills, she would be the first to know.

Arthur was enjoying a rare solitary late afternoon sitting in his chair beside his cottage window with Fluffy on his lap. 'We've come a long way, Fluffy. The village is buzzing – new shops and visitors *and* most of my family back home. Now, there's a thought. Hannah's been very quiet these last five years; we're lucky to get a card at Christmas from her. I know she's a busy lawyer in Dubai, but it would be good for her to come home to see the changes to the village. It's her 30th in September; we should arrange a party. Hannah always loved a party.'

Arthur raised his eyebrows at the sight of Tabitha and Tallulah, then Matilda and Cindy going into the Post Office & General Store laden with bags. The sign on the door was turned from "OPEN" to "CLOSED". Mrs Carruthers had initiated a "lock-in".

'Hello girls, I'm so excited! A ladies' gathering has been well overdue.' Mrs Carruthers grabbed her Tarot Cards and Ouija Board. 'Hopefully, you've raided David Makepeace's wine cellar, I can see you've come fully supplied with nibbles. Now off you go upstairs to

Theo's old apartment, we won't be disturbed up there.'

Arthur's interest was aroused, the light went on in the upstairs apartment, he could see the girls chatting and dancing around. Within seconds he heard a shot. The girls disappeared from view, and a man stood in the window; a bald man holding a gun.

In the blink of an eye, another man flew across the road, kicked down the door of the Post Office & General Store and ran inside. There were now two men in the apartment window with punches being thrown. Arthur rushed towards his front door and dragged the sack of pebbles he'd collected earlier in the day out onto the High Street. He gave his loudest whistle bringing Theo and David Makepeace running to his aid followed by several other members of the community. They helped Arthur pour the pebbles over the front step of the Post Office & General Store. Arthur stood tall. 'Backs to the wall everyone. Get ready to pounce once the pebbles have done their job.'

Minutes later, the bald intruder ran out of the shop and skidded on the pebbles. He fell face first onto the pavement and knocked his head on the kerb. Fluffy jumped on top of the limp body and stood guard. Arthur scratched his chin. 'Well, that was easier than I thought.'

*

It was time to reflect in the King Arthur that evening. Bruce Copperfield couldn't take his eyes off Tallulah, who was relishing his attention. 'So, when did you decide to act like a member of the SAS? Breaking down doors and bringing a criminal to his knees right in front of a room full of damsels in distress.'

'I've not been far away, Tallulah. I've been keeping an eye on you to make sure you and the baby are OK.'

Tallulah's green eyes widened. 'Oh, have you now? Well, I'll forgive you for deserting me.' She gave Bruce a sideways glance. 'It was a false alarm anyway.'

The door to the King Arthur flew open and a group of reporters and camera crew bundled in. 'Any chance of some rooms for the night and a bite to eat? We're here to do some filming in the morning for a slot on the national news. Quite a reputation this place has been getting.'

All eyes turned to Theo, what an opportunity for the new Head of Tourism. Theo flashed his best smile. 'Certainly, ladies and gentlemen. We have several different types of accommodation from which you may choose. I think it's always best to sample what's on offer before reporting back to the general public via the national news. Let me offer you some drinks first, on the house of course.'

*

It was a sunny morning when Clive stepped out of his helicopter; Leticia had given him the "heads up" about the Press filming in the village. It was only a short journey from the helipad to the village centre by chauffeur-driven Bentley. 'Good morning, ladies and gentlemen, what a pleasure it is to welcome you all to Truelove Hills. If you would like to take any aerial shots, then my helicopter is at your disposal.'

Mrs Carruthers was being interviewed by one of the reporters. 'Of course, the village is a place for romance. You only have to look at our name. What? What do you mean? How can I back that up? Well, we can arrange marriages for a start.'

The reporter turned his attention to Lady Lovett. 'My chateau is the perfect wedding venue. What? You're asking if we have a matchmaking facility? I'm not quite sure what you mean.'

Clive raised his eyebrows at Arthur and Arthur winked back. 'Let *me* go and talk to those reporters.'

Arthur stood in the centre of the village square and whistled to gain attention. 'Truelove Hills is a village with the biggest heart you will ever find. When you come to stay here, from wherever you are in the world, you will experience a holiday like no other. You see, it's all about the pebbles.' Arthur reached into his pocket and held up a pebble heart. 'And if you are lucky enough to receive one of these, the spirit of Truelove Hills will be with you wherever you go.'

The village fell silent, and Arthur noticed the red light still on the camera, so he kept talking. 'The path of true love doesn't always run smoothly; it sometimes needs a bit of help. If there's anyone here today who has already identified their true love but things need speeding up then come to see me, and I will personally engrave a pebble heart for you to help you on your way.'

There were cheers from the film crew. 'It's a wrap! Great work, Mr Makepeace. This is a truly amazing place. There's a good chance the film will go global, get ready for the influx of tourists.'

*

The residents of Truelove Hills watched the evening news in the lounge bar of the King Arthur. Those aerial shots were the icing on the cake.

Clive slapped Arthur on the back. 'I can't believe you had to engrave seven hearts before the Press would return to London! I quite like the idea of arranged marriages, that was a good one by Mrs Carruthers.'

Arthur chuckled. 'She meant to say "weddings" not "marriages". We can arrange weddings, not marriages, we're not matchmakers. The conversation was getting a bit hairy before I had to step in and get all mushy.'

Clive's eyes twinkled. 'I'd like to do a bit of matchmaking and arrange a marriage.'

Theo's phone kept beeping. 'Well, it looks like you'll get a chance, Clive. I'm starting to get enquiries about our "matchmaking" events.'

Leticia couldn't help but overhear. 'I'd be happy to

host such events at Chateau Amore de Pebblio.'

Arthur raised his eyes to the ceiling, another one of Mrs Carruthers' indiscretions that was turning out to be nothing but an unnecessary distraction. The telephone behind the bar was ringing, and with no-one choosing to answer it, Arthur decided to take the call.

'Grandpa, it's Hannah! I've just seen you on the television, you were amazing.'

'Hannah! I was thinking about you yesterday. You need to come home for your birthday this year because we're having a party. Make sure you book your flights in good time, the party won't be the same without you. I'm sorry, Hannah, there's such a noise going on in the pub that I'm struggling to hear. See you in September. I'll let everyone know you're coming home.'

Arthur rubbed his hands together. Hannah had watched him on the TV in Dubai – confirmation that the news story *had* gone global.

24

MATCHMAKING AT THE CHATEAU

The late August Bank Holiday Weekend had taken on a new meaning in Truelove Hills; it was the first time the village had hosted a matchmaking event and, with 30 single hopefuls arriving on Saturday morning, it was all hands on deck to ensure the weekend was a success.

Leticia and Clive had prepared an agenda and the plan for the weekend was as follows:

SATURDAY

10.00 – Tour of the village and its facilities

12.00 – Lunch at Cindy's Bistro

2.00 – Speed dating in the chateau's grand hall

8.00 – Dinner on the chateau terrace

SUNDAY

9.00 – Village hike

11.00 – Brunch at the King Arthur

4.00 – Makeover session by Lady Lovett

8.00 – Barbecue at Pebble Peak

10.00 – Fireworks at the chateau

MONDAY

10.00 – Compatibility questionnaire

12.00 – Compatibility results

Mrs Carruthers held the agenda at arm's length and sniffed loudly before finishing her morning cappuccino at Cindy's Bakery. 'If Leticia and Clive think they're going to get a marriage arranged this weekend then they've got another think coming. It takes time to get to know someone; you can't just get marriages sorted on the spot. Look at me, I'm 72 now and still waiting for the right man to come along. All this matchmaking stuff is pie in the sky; ridiculous idea if you ask me.'

Cindy smiled brightly. 'It was *your* idea, Mrs Carruthers, admittedly in a roundabout way. Sometimes you need to think before you speak it can cause all sorts of trouble for the people around you.'

Mrs Carruthers stood up. 'I need to get back to my shop. Tabitha's only covering for half an hour. If you're still sour with me about confusing Jamie Sonning-Smythe with Jamie Thistlewaite, then that's your loss. As far as I'm concerned, both Jamie's are good for nothings; one's back in prison and we don't see the other one from one month to the next.'

'Well, I'm sorry to disappoint you, Mrs Carruthers, but Jamie's booked a Glamping hut for this weekend, and we're finally going to have our picnic on Saturday night; the picnic you put a stop to in June.'

Mrs Carruthers tore up the agenda and shoved it in the bin before marching out of the bakery with her eyes to the floor.

*

Saturday's events were well underway before one of the singles excused himself from the speed dating session. He'd seen more to his liking during the village tour in the morning than was available now at the chateau. All of the singles were young or middle-aged and being in his seventies he felt out of place. The door to the Post Office & General Store flew open just before closing time.

'Mrs Carruthers isn't it? My name's Eric and, I know it's very fast of me, but I wondered if you would be available to go for a drink in the King Arthur this evening? At our time of life, there's no time to waste.'

Mrs Carruthers fluttered her eyelashes and twisted a lock of her wiry grey hair around a finger. 'Well, I am partial to the occasional brandy, double of course.'

Eric clapped in delight. 'I'll collect you at seven, then maybe after a drink we could go for a bite to eat at Cindy's Bistro.'

Mrs Carruthers managed a nod and a wave before locking Eric out of the shop. What a stroke of luck; Cindy would be up at Pebble Peak tonight, she wouldn't find out about her date with the short, grey and enthusiastic Eric.

*

Jamie popped a champagne cork, Cindy would be here in less than ten minutes. He'd been dreaming of this day. There was something different about the girl with a conscience who put everyone before herself. She was wholesome and pure, a goddess if ever there was one and he could hear her footsteps outside the Summer hut door.

'Cindy, you're finally here!' Jamie kissed her on both cheeks.

Cindy snorted before climbing on the bed and rolling around in hysterics. 'Have you seen the Compatibility Questionnaire they're using on Monday? Your father popped by this afternoon and handed me one. He said it wouldn't harm if I gave it a go.'

Jamie reached on top of the fridge. 'You mean this? Papa's left one for me too.'

Cindy took hold of the glass of champagne Jamie offered her and gulped it down in two. 'Well, you know what we need to do. We need to complete the questionnaires, hand them in and see if we win.'

'What will we win?'

'A helicopter ride over Truelove Hills and a discounted wedding at the chateau.'

Jamie's eyelashes were far too long for his own good, and Cindy's stomach somersaulted when his turquoise eyes held her gaze. 'How about we cheat?'

'Yes! Let's do it. We'll compare our answers to get the perfect match!'

*

On Sunday there was a poor turnout for the village hike and brunch. Still, it had been a late night on Saturday, and many of the singles had taken the opportunity for a lie in. Lady Lovett's makeover session wasn't that popular either. The barbecue at Pebble Peak provided a good turnout. Arthur ventured up there with Fluffy and a basket full of hearts, by ten o'clock he had nine orders for personalised engravings and as he strolled back down the High Street to his cottage, the fireworks erupted. Fluffy let out a yelp and Arthur picked him up. 'There's nothing to worry about, Fluffy. They're only pretty lights. From what I've seen tonight, you'll need to get used to fireworks. I think Clive and Leticia have got a good thing going with this matchmaking stuff, don't tell them I told you mind.'

*

On Monday, it was questionnaire time. Clive stood next to the piano in the grand hall of the chateau to announce the results. He fiddled with his tie and ran a finger under his collar. 'Well, this is a surprise, I'm quite taken aback.'

Jamie squeezed Cindy's waist.

'The most compatible couple in Truelove Hills this weekend is . . . Eric Brimstone and Ida Carruthers.'

Cindy's mouth fell open as Mrs Carruthers walked up to the piano on the arm of Eric Brimstone. She curtseyed in front of Clive and grabbed the envelope he was holding containing details of the prize. 'I would like to thank Lord Sonning-Smythe and Lady Lovett for arranging this weekend. It has been nothing short of magical. Eric and I would never have met but for my original idea of arranged marriages as part of the village offering.'

Jamie started a round of applause, and Clive edged over to his side. 'It was a draw, Jamie. I couldn't very well announce that my son had won the prize, could I? I hoped you and Cindy would both complete a questionnaire, but I didn't realise how compatible you are. She's a keeper, Jamie, don't ever let her go.'

25

HANNAH'S RETURN

Saturday the 7th of September had arrived, and there was no sign of Hannah. Tallulah stood on a bar stool at the King Arthur and secured the birthday bunting to the oak beams on the ceiling of the lounge bar. Matilda and Tabitha blew up balloons, and David Makepeace had a sinking feeling. 'Your sister hasn't been home for five years. She's far too busy in Dubai. There's no way she's going to turn up today for a birthday party. Your grandfather is living in cloud cuckoo land.'

At seven o'clock Hannah climbed out of a taxi on the outskirts of the village, she knew all the alleyways and shortcuts to the High Street. She just hoped that Mrs Carruthers was in, she had never needed her more.

Eight o'clock and the pub was alive. Arthur had asked David to arrange a DJ, and the outside of the

King Arthur was now adorned with "30 Today!", "Birthday Girl!" banners. There was even a blown-up photograph of Hannah when she was a baby, and another when she was ten. Her graduation photo took pride of place on the bar.

Arthur looked at his watch. 'She'll be here in a minute; she won't let me down.'

Sure enough, two minutes past eight and the pub door opened to the welcome sight of Hannah. She hadn't changed a bit in the last five years. Her black curly hair hung half-way down her back, and she rushed over to hug her grandfather first. 'You really have a way with you, Grandpa. When you set your mind to something, it always happens.'

'My little Hannah. You're a sight for sore eyes. I can't believe you watched me on the TV in Dubai. Things have changed so much around here, and I want you to take part in the new Truelove Hills experience, it isn't the same with you over on the other side of the world.'

Hannah took hold of her grandfather's hand. 'You need to sit down, Grandpa, there's something I have to tell you.'

Arthur felt the importance in Hannah's tone, and her sisters and father crowded around to hear her news. 'When we spoke on the phone in July, I wasn't in Dubai.'

David Makepeace interrupted. 'I told you that, Dad, it was too late for Hannah to be up when she made the call. She wouldn't have phoned from Dubai at two in the morning.'

Arthur coughed. 'But you said you saw me on the TV.'

'I know, Grandpa. I certainly did, but I was already back in the UK at the time. I wanted to come home, but I didn't know how to tell you. I didn't want you to think that I'd failed, I needed to get my own law firm established so that I can work independently with hours to suit me and AJ.'

Hannah held up her hand to signal to the DJ to stop the music. 'Just wait here a minute while I go and find Mrs Carruthers.'

Hannah returned holding the hand of a small, curly haired boy. 'This is AJ, it's short for Arthur Junior, and he's four years' old. Before you ask any questions, I'll answer them. AJ doesn't have a father; he was a gift to me at my graduation party; you all know how much I used to love to party. He's the best thing in my life, and I'm sure he'll brighten your lives too.'

Hannah turned to her father. 'I'll fill you in with all the details tomorrow, Daddy, you've gone to so much trouble to arrange my party that I want us all to enjoy it.'

Arthur patted his knee. 'Come over here, AJ, have

a little sit on your great-grandfather so that we can get to know each other.'

AJ ran over to Arthur and hugged him with all his might. 'The boy's a Makepeace all right. Spitting image of his mother; no mistaking it. Clive, are you ready for our next project? We need to refurbish the old school. It should be modern inside with a pebblestone exterior. Young AJ here will be one of the first pupils, and if he's anything like his mum, he'll be a shining star.' Hannah smiled at the DJ, and the music started up again.

Jamie lifted AJ from Arthur's knee. 'Come on little man, Theo and I will show you some robot moves and a bit of breakdancing.' AJ giggled, his little round face shining with delight.

Matilda was annoyed with her sister. 'Why didn't you tell us, Hannah? You disappeared for five years. We could have helped you and AJ.'

Hannah sighed. 'You were all at important stages in your lives and, besides, I keep thinking about our mother's letter. For a long time, I felt such a failure.'

'I haven't read that letter for years. I can't even remember what it says.'

Hannah reached into her bag and handed Matilda a copy. 'I can't see anything in here that you need to worry about, in fact, I think our mother was very wise. She writes: "*The world is at your feet, Hannah, please take it in both hands and let nothing or no-one hold you back."* That's what you're doing now; you're following her guidance.'

Hannah took the letter back. 'Let's see what advice she gave you: "*I wish you a life full of happiness and fulfilment and that whatever path you venture down is the right one; only you will know when it's right.*" Does that ring true with you?'

Matilda gulped. 'Definitely. I went off on the wrong path to New York, but with a bit of help from Grandpa and Theo I found the right path in the end. What did mother say about the twins?'

'She said: "*double the trouble, double the fun!*".' Hannah and Matilda stared at each other and then burst into laughter.

Tabitha and Tallulah were now spinning AJ around on the small dancefloor. Tallulah picked him up and took him over to the buffet table. 'Now, no-one is looking, if you poke your finger into a bit of the cream you can be the first one to try Mummy's birthday cake. I won't tell. Go on; I dare you.'

Matilda linked arms with Hannah. 'My nephew is so adorable. I want to pick him up and swing him around from here until eternity.'

Hannah laughed. 'He's getting a bit heavy for that. Besides, I understand that Theo has already requested that you stand by his side from here until eternity.'

Matilda blushed. 'Well, Theo's very lucky. It was a

rubbish proposal.' Matilda held up her hand to show Hannah her ring. 'At least he made a bit of an effort with the ring.'

Hannah's eyes widened at the sight of the large solitaire diamond. 'Do you have any dates in mind for your wedding?'

Matilda's eyes shone. 'I have a very special date in mind.'

Clive chuckled as he brought another pint over to Arthur. 'Is there any reason why your great-grandson has got cream on his nose *and* in his hair?' Clive raised his pint glass and clinked it with his friend's. 'May Truelove Hills be blessed with many more little "AJ's". We'll need a few more children to fill our school. I suggest we start work on the project next week. To the next generation, Arthur, to the next generation!'

It was midnight before Arthur pushed open the door to his cottage, Fluffy went trotting in, but Arthur stood outside looking up at the sky. 'What a turn up for the books, Alice, we're great-grandparents.' Fluffy came looking for his master. 'I've nearly finished, Fluffy.' Arthur looked to the sky again, if Mrs Carruthers was watching him talking to himself, he didn't care, this was too important. 'Harriet, if you can hear me you should be very proud of your girls, very proud indeed.'

26

HANNAH'S HOUSE

A private family brunch in the King Arthur was hastily arranged for the morning after Hannah's party. Hannah had some explaining to do, and David Makepeace was not in the least bit forgiving.

'What I can't understand, Hannah, is why you couldn't confide in *any* member of your family. If you couldn't talk to me, you have three sisters. I've been a grandfather for four years, and I didn't even know. Do you realise how that makes me feel?'

Tears pricked Hannah's eyes, and she turned around to search for AJ who was playing happily with Theo in the back garden of the pub.

'I'm so sorry, Daddy, I didn't want to bring more trauma on the family. It was hard enough losing our mother. You, Grandma and Grandpa gave up so much to raise us, things were settling down with all of us gaining qualifications and moving away. It was your time to relax and enjoy yourselves. I couldn't let you know that one silly mistake had changed my life; I couldn't burden you with my problems until I had found a way around them.'

Arthur wiped his mouth on a napkin before placing it on his plate and pushing back his chair. 'What's done is done. Hannah was in a very difficult situation but she's sorted it out now and a very fine job she's done with the newest member of our family. I'm off out the back to play footie with AJ and Theo, come along girls, let's leave Hannah and your father to have a bit of alone time.'

Tabitha and Tallulah carried a tray of teas and coffees out into the garden and sat down with Matilda who was watching the boys kick a soft ball between two chairs erected as makeshift goalposts, with the help of Fluffy.

Tabitha poured the tea. 'You look thoughtful, Tilly.'

'I am, Tabitha. I suppose we're all in shock about Hannah's news. Where do you think she'll live with AJ?'

Tallulah sipped her coffee. 'I'm sure she's got loads of money saved up. She always had the heaviest piggy bank when we were growing up, and now that she's a lawyer she'll be earning a fortune.'

Matilda slid along the wooden bench seat to make room for her grandfather to sit down. 'We were just wondering where Hannah will live with AJ. Tallulah says she won't be short of money, but there are no houses for sale in Truelove Hills. Do you think they'll buy somewhere in one of the surrounding villages?'

Arthur reached for a chocolate biscuit. 'Good point, Matilda, good point. I'll need to speak to Clive about the shortage of housing in the village.'

Tabitha helped herself to a biscuit too. 'I suppose they could always stay in the apartment above the Post Office & General Store, or even in one of the rooms in the guest house; they stayed there last night.'

Arthur placed his biscuit on the tray and wandered off.

The girls watched as he shut the gate to the pub garden behind him and headed off up the hill towards Pebble Peak.

Tallulah tutted. 'Surely Grandpa's not thinking about putting them up in the Glamping huts? They'll be freezing in the winter.'

Forty-five minutes later, Arthur was back. 'Is Hannah still talking to her father?'

Hannah and David strolled into the garden arm in arm. 'Where have you been, Grandpa? We saw you marching off up the hill. You were in such a hurry that you forgot to take Fluffy with you; he's been keeping watch at the gate.'

Arthur bent down to pat Fluffy. 'Well, it looks like you two have sorted out your differences. That's good; that's good.'

Matilda could tell when her grandfather was thinking as he was speaking. He was undoubtedly on a mission about something. 'What have you done now, Grandpa?'

Arthur sat down and lifted Fluffy onto his lap. 'When I was a young boy, I had a friend at the castle called Billy Tomlin. He was in the same class as Alice and me. It was before Alice became the apple of my eye and I used to go and play with Billy at his house after school.'

Everyone was intrigued to hear Arthur's latest tale. 'I thought Billy's house was the best in Pebblestown. I wished I lived there. We had many adventures in that house.'

Tallulah shrugged her shoulders. 'So, you used to play with a boy who lived in Lady Leticia's "castle" as you call it. We all know it's the best "house" in the village. What's new?'

Arthur shook his head. 'No, that's not what I mean. My friend's house was in the grounds of the castle, right down the bottom, on the side of the hill overlooking the sea. His mother was the housekeeper there. It had access to a private beach that the castle's previous owners called Pebble Cove. Not much sand on that beach; mainly pebbles.'

Matilda was intrigued. 'I never knew there was a house in the grounds of the chateau.'

Arthur stroked Fluffy, still in thinking mode. 'Not many people do. It's been empty since Leticia and her husband bought the place. You can't see it unless you're in the air or on the water.' AJ climbed onto the bench and lifted Fluffy off Arthur's lap. 'Anyway, I've just spoken to Leticia, and she'd be up for Hannah taking the house off her hands. She'd sell it for a reasonable price and help with sorting out private access so that AJ doesn't disturb the flowerbeds at the castle or damage any of the statues. I thought that was fair of her.'

Hannah clapped her hands. 'It sounds wonderful, Grandpa! When can we see the house?'

'Well, "Hannah's House" will be available for viewing this afternoon. I suggest we all go and take a look. I can fill you in with a few stories I've heard about it; to do with smugglers and the like.'

AJ and Fluffy ran off to play with the ball, and Arthur picked up the chocolate biscuit, this was the reaction he'd hoped for. Once Hannah had seen the house, she wouldn't want to live anywhere else.

*

The Makepeace family stood outside the derelict

single-storey building, and Hannah's face dropped.

Arthur rubbed his hands together. 'Leticia will be here in a minute. Leave it to me to do the negotiating; we don't want her to think we're over keen and that it's a done deal.'

Lady Leticia tried several keys before she found the right one to open the front door. Arthur and Theo helped by holding back the gnarled branches of an overgrown wisteria. 'I do believe that I've never set foot inside this little house. I left all the property management issues to my husband. I'd forgotten it was even here down the edge of a cliff.'

Hannah picked AJ up and entered the empty shell of a former home. 'Grandpa, this place isn't habitable. It's certainly not somewhere to raise a child.'

Arthur patted Hannah on the back and whispered in her ear. 'That's good, Hannah. Keep going.'

'I mean it, Grandpa, we need somewhere to live *now*. This house needs a lot of work doing to it'. I can't see anyone wanting to buy it.'

David Makepeace wiped his sleeve on a window overlooking the sea. 'I can't see any access to a private beach.'

Leticia huffed. 'My husband always said the private beach wasn't worth having; that it's nothing more than a small stretch of pebbles, not even enough room for a sunbed. We never bothered going down there; the sun's not good for the skin. Well, now that I've opened the door, I'll leave you to have a look around. Lock up when you've finished and drop the keys back at the chateau.'

Arthur waited until the coast was clear, then made his way into the kitchen. 'Follow me, everyone. I'll show you the way to the beach.'

On Arthur's instruction, David and Theo prised open a door in the floor next to the kitchen sink. Arthur sat on the eroding concrete and lowered his legs into the cavity. 'There are only ninety-nine shallow steps with a nice sturdy handrail. Come on everyone; we're off to the beach!'

Opening the door that led to the beach was more straightforward than Arthur had hoped. It was only bolted from the inside. The tide was out, the sun was shining and the Makepeace's all stepped out of the secret access route to survey Pebble Cove.

Matilda breathed in the sea air. 'This place is amazing! You *have* to buy it, Hannah. We'll have our own private family beach!'

Tabitha and Tallulah ran over the pebbles to the water's edge, their curly red hair flying behind them; Fluffy was already yapping happily in the sea.

Hannah watched as AJ and Theo tried to skim stones on the calm waters of the cove, she glanced at her father who was having an in-depth discussion with

Arthur. As a lawyer, her mind was racing. The house needed a lot of work, but if she could do a deal with Lady Lovett to buy it with Pebble Cove thrown in, and with a private access route from the main road to the property along the edge of the chateau grounds, it would work well for all parties.

AJ shrieked with delight. 'Mummy! Mummy! I can see a crab, and I've found you a shell!'

Arthur shouted back to AJ. 'Keep looking, son. There are lots of rock pools in Pebble Cove, you'll find a fish or two in a minute. I'll bring you a net and bucket next time we come, I've got some in my shed.'

Hannah suppressed a chuckle at her grandfather's blatant manipulation before calling out to him. 'Keep an eye on AJ, Grandpa. I'm going to see Lady Lovett.'

Leticia was in the chateau's rose garden, pruning shears in hand. 'I've been thinking, Hannah, you're quite correct in stating that the house needs renovating. If it helps, I could offer you discounted accommodation at the chateau until the work is complete.'

Hannah went into negotiation mode. 'That's very kind of you, Lady Lovett, but the renovation work will cost a fortune, I'll need to save every penny I earn from now until eternity to pay for it, my mortgage will be huge. AJ and I will need to stay with family to cut down on costs until the property is habitable. If I were to make you an offer, is it correct that Pebble Cove will be included and that private access to the house will be granted along the edge of the chateau's grounds?'

Leticia took off her gardening gloves. 'I am sure we can come to an arrangement. Come with me into the chateau, and we can talk business.'

*

One hour – and two cappuccinos – later, Hannah returned to her family with the news. 'You're all now standing on the Makepeace family's private beach! I've shaken hands with Lady Lovett, and the house is mine. We'll need to stay with whoever can put us up for the next few months; the renovations won't be completed until early in the New Year, but once we've moved in, I'll return the favour; there'll be lots of parties in "Hannah's House".'

Arthur held his hand to his chest and winked up at the sky. He blew his nose and startled Fluffy. Arthur bent down to give the dog a treat. 'That's between us, Fluffy. There's no more time to be sad. This is a new beginning, and I have an excellent feeling that from now on we're all going to be very happy indeed . . .'

EPILOGUE

Christmas Eve, 2019

Cindy wiped away a tear as she trudged up the High Street in her wellies. The snow was deep in Truelove Hills, but it was even worse in Europe, and all flights to the UK from Spain had been cancelled. Cindy's parents had telephoned yesterday to advise that they wouldn't make it home for Christmas. Still, these things happen, and there was so much to do this morning that Cindy didn't have time to dwell on what might have been. When she reached Chateau Amore de Pebblio, she was ushered inside and taken upstairs for breakfast with Matilda.

*

Four hours later and the chateau was a hive of activity. Tabitha and Tallulah stood on the landing looking down into the grand hallway. Tallulah tutted as a curly red tendril escaped the neat chignon the hairdresser had spent ages pinning in place. 'Why on earth anyone would want to get married on Christmas Eve amazes me. There are so many other days in the year when it's warm and not so busy, Christmas sucks for a wedding.'

Hannah ventured onto the landing with AJ and Fluffy. AJ held the dog's crystal-adorned lead, and Hannah held her son's hand.

Lord Sonning-Smythe was in his element playing Christmas tunes on the piano in the black and white marble hallway, and the large floor to ceiling arched windows gave the guests a stunning view of the heavy snowfall that had encompassed the village overnight.

Steve and Bruce Copperfield joined Tabitha and Tallulah at the top of the stairs, followed by Matilda and David Makepeace. Clive changed the tune to "Silent Night", and Hannah, AJ and Fluffy made their way down the stairs first, followed by Tabitha and Tallulah with bouquets in hand. They were half-way down when David squeezed Tilly's hand. 'You make such a beautiful bride. Your mother and grandmother would be so proud of you, it's twenty years to the day you know.' Tilly nodded, and the bride and her father began their descent.

Cindy then appeared at the top of the stairs and linked arms with her brothers. With the Makepeace family now in the hallway, the second bride could begin her walk to married life.

Theo and Jamie stood in front of the Registrar, and Mrs Carruthers blew her nose loudly. She turned to Lady Leticia. 'This is all too much, two of our girls married in one go. Who would ever have believed it less than a year ago?' Eric reached into his pocket and handed Mrs Carruthers his starched white handkerchief; he guessed she would make good use of it. His primary responsibility for the afternoon was to avoid squashing the cardboard confetti boxes that Mrs Carruthers had found in the General Store. They were faded and fragile; there had been no weddings in Truelove Hills for a generation.

Clive slipped into the seat next to Arthur and grabbed his friend's arm before whispering, 'Another mission accomplished.'

Arthur's attention turned to the enormous snowflakes dancing around outside. When he was a young boy, he loved the snow; there was sledging, snowball fights and snowmen with coal for eyes and carrots for noses. When the girls were young, Alice always knitted a few spare hats and scarves for the snowmen. On the worst weather days, the school was closed; now there was a thought . . . AJ would love that! There was so much to look forward to.

Clive couldn't contain his secret any longer, and he whispered to Arthur again. 'I'm going to be a grandfather.'

Arthur's heart leapt, and he squeezed his friend's hand tightly. 'It's the best job in the world Clive, trust me, it's the best job in the world!'

****

Now available in the Truelove Hills series!

TRUELOVE HILLS

Mystery at Pebble Cove

The truth always prevails — with some exceptions . . .

When esteemed lawyer Hannah Makepeace and her four-year-old son move into a former smugglers' hideaway, little do they know that their lives will become entwined in events that happened at Pebble Cove over a century ago.

Tobias Finchinglake is Hannah's first client when she returns to Truelove Hills from Dubai. He has no idea how their connection will lead to unravelling a mystery surrounding his ancestry that has plagued him all his life.

Secrets are uncovered at Chateau Amore de Pebblio, Sonning Hall and Finchinglake Vineyard. Hannah's grandfather knows more than most. Will Arthur Makepeace reveal the missing piece of the jigsaw? Or will he keep the biggest secret of his life?

Printed in Great Britain
by Amazon